CW01020699

Roger Dale Watson Jr. is a husband and a father of five children. He spent most of his life as a corrections officer. He enjoys spending time with his family as well as writing; he enjoys entertaining a reader and thanks them for the time they take out of their lives to enjoy his work.

I dedicate this to my wife, Carla Watson, and our children: Kayle Babineaux, Christina Buteau, Roger Watson 3rd, Dillon Watson, and Madison Buteau.

Roger Dale Watson Jr.

CRIES OF INNOCENCE

AUSTIN MACAULEY PUBLISHERS™

LONDON • CAMBRIDGE • NEW YORK • SHARJAH

Ordering Information:
Quantity sales: special discounts are available on quantity purchases by corporations, associations, and others. For details, contact the publisher at the address below.

Publisher's Cataloging-in-Publication data
Watson Jr., Roger Dale
Cries of Innocence

ISBN 9781643783864 (Paperback)
ISBN 9781643783871 (Hardback)
ISBN 9781645367659 (ePub e-book)

Library of Congress Control Number: 2019916438

The main category of the book — FICTION / General

www.austinmacauley.com/us

First Published (2019)
Austin Macauley Publishers LLC
40 Wall Street, 28th Floor
New York, NY 10005
USA

mail-usa@austinmacauley.com
+1 (646) 5125767

Thank you God for the talent you have gifted me with—to take the words in my head and put them on paper to entertain people of all ages.

Introduction

This is an intriguing and dramatic story of losses, gains, and the true meaning of sticking together.
It is a story of events that spun out of control.

A tragedy strikes a group of small town girls unexpectedly, causing the death of Hollie's father. It sends them on a journey that takes four young teens on a path that will not only test their friendship and their ability to stay together as a group but cause them to grow up with the scares of life and the will to fight to stay alive.
Being tested with loyalty, romance, adventure, lies, corruption, death, and the love that kept them together as girls may be the same thing they may have to kill to protect as women or die trying.

Chapter 1

Unfolding of the Journey

The past year of my life hasn't been as bad as I think. I thought this was a retirement home but it turned out to be quite well. The family property got too much for me to take care of. So I moved into my little room on Ward 26 East Wing, that is where I call home now. It's a cozy little place and the nurses are very friendly. Although their pill carts get kind of annoying with their squeaky wheels, it's funny what one can get used to. But I've got a few things to look forward to; the food is great, so is the company, and my grandson comes to see me on the first Wednesday of every month and we have lunch, ohhh how I look forward to that! Every lunch with my grandson starts and ends basically the same way or at least that's what I thought, this particular Wednesday took me back to a time in my life when I was in my prime.

"Hello, my name is Hollie Chapman, and this is my story. Hello life, good morning sunshine, it's going to be a beautiful day." The warmth from the sun and the bright of the day reminds me that I didn't lower my blinds last night.

"Hello, Miss Hollie, you haven't started talking to yourself, have you, love?"

"No dear, just talking to the day. I forgot to lower my blinds last night and that sun is so bright. Nurse Betty, you snuck up on me with that cart."

"No, Miss Hollie, it's the same cart, we just got a new set of wheels (laughing). No more squeaky cart for me."

"Besides, Miss Hollie, did you forget what day it is? It's Wednesday, ya' know its lunch date with that handsome of yours." As the warm sun crossed my face and the cool water from the sink touched my hands, I remembered what today was. But I didn't know then, at that one moment in time, that the next 24 hours would be the longest 24 hours of my life.

Just as fast as the conversation started with Nurse Betty, just like that she was gone again. My room grew quiet and I was left with my own thoughts as I stared into the mirror looking at how age had taken over my body. My knees just weren't what they used to be is what I'm reminded of when I lace up my shoes. My train of thought was interrupted by the sound of the door opening and the voice of my grandson. "Hey, pretty lady, you ready for our lunch date?"

"Oh, Dillon, for a minute you had me thinking I was in the wrong room."

With a crisp young man's voice, he replies, "Granny, no matter how old you feel, you'll always be my best girl. By the way, where do you want to go hangout today?"

"Now you know anywhere with you is a place I wanna be. But if I can pick a place, I wanna go to the old place

11

where you used to go to when you were a lil' boy, do you remember where that is?"

You would have thought I took his breath away and as he gathered what breath he could, he replayed, "Now, Granny, you know I'll never forget our tree table and tree swing, those were the best summers of my life at that old house. But what has you wanting to go back there?"

"Oh, just been thinking about life and how it was back then, things were so slow and it was truly a better time."

"Yea, Granny, it was even for me. And if that's what you want, for sure we can go there." And just like that we were off, I knew I only had checked out a pass for just a few hours but who would miss a simple old lady anyway. So we were off on the way to the open road and only stopped to fuel up and get a drink for the road. I know my grandson always has a lot to say but when he climbed in, I told him as long as he drove, I would talk, and boy did I have a lot to say. For years I was heartbroken and was asked a lot of questions about my past by my son and even my grandson and today I felt like telling him the things I'd been staying away from for a long time.

So with the window down and the wind in my face, we took off. "Granny, since you are in such a talking mood, how 'bout telling me about who I am and who we are, I mean not as a person but as a family. To some we are law enforcement and to some we are below thugs."

As I heard him talk, I realized that he had lived through my past and my present as well as his father and my closest three friends as well. We talked, him and I, as we hadn't done in a long time. He drove as I rambled about how I grew up in our neighborhood hanging out in our little group. We were four young girls who were far from any gang in reality, but in our own head we were a tight-knit group all the same. I told him of our past like it was an action movie and how we were out late riding bikes all day for what felt like hours away from home and only being a few blocks away at any given time. Our local park was our hideout spot between sleepovers and summer nights. Carla Ann, she was our brainiac and most of the time the glue that held us together. She was of a calm nature and could settle down any spat we had. Now Kayle on the other hand, she was the hot-blooded one. She was a 'in your face' and a 'tell it like it was' kinda girl (laughing). She was the bravest girl I'd ever known. And the same bravery that would protect us is usually what got us in trouble.

From the elders screaming (get off their lawn) to the neighborhood boys trying to kick us off the town's baseball field on a Saturday morning. But the most humorous of it all was how she stood up to the bullies. She wasn't scared of anything. Now Madison on the other hand, she was the chicken (chuckling), she was the nervous one and I kinda felt closer to her maybe because we both shared the loss of our mother at such an early age. Like her it was just my dad and I as far back as I can remember. I never really knew my mom as she passed giving birth to me. She got to know her mom but just briefly as she was very ill and passed in her sleep when she was just five. She remembers the feel of a mother's hand that I never felt, the smell after a hug during the day that I never got, the pat on the back for a job well done, or a kiss goodnight; all I never got, so I found myself living my own memories in her stories about her and her own mom.

Now my father and I were okay being alone. I guess being alone was all we ever knew. Dad traveled a lot being in politics, he was here today and gone tomorrow, so I spent a lot of my youth with Carla and her family. We spent our every available moment together. I loved my dad so much, he was my everything, my whole world. My dad and I did everything together, I never felt out of place standing in the bait store with all the dads and their sons getting supplies to start a day of fishing. And I never knew where or how he got the answers to all my thousand girl questions but he would sit and listen to my every problem whether it was a spat between our group or why does this boy pick on me and all the wheres and whys I could come up with. He would just sit and be so supportive of me. Oh how I still love and miss him.

He hired a nanny and that was when I came into womanhood, I guess that was too much for him to handle (laughing). He never ran from any problem and he led by example, he never asked more from me than he himself was willing to give and never lost his temper with me when I couldn't catch on right away. He would just simply say, "Now, Button, that's it for tonight, let's hit it in the A.M." Each of us brought our own uniqueness to our group. And seemed to be just the glue to hold it together, we all had emotional gaps from our childhood to our early teens. We all had hardworking dads so we shared the only two moms in our group. They stepped up and looked after us and helped us through some really hard times. My dad would be gone for weeks at a time and he took his work very seriously. And when we were together, he took that time just as serious, we were very close, he was my best friend.

Chapter 2

The Dance

I know about traditions and I know how deep they can run in a small town, there was a tradition in our town that I will never forget. It was something that I had seen families attend for as long as I can remember. It was our daddy-daughter dance at our high school. It was a time the whole town looked forward to, stores closed early, dads took off work, and if you were the young girl that was able to attend, it was a time you were no longer seen as a child. To outsiders it was just a school dance but to our little town it was a tribute to fathers and daughters and a passage from childhood into the first stage of being noticed as a young woman. It was the start of being able to be left alone, babysitting jobs, and the local super market owner would hire you to work after school and on weekends. It was a ninth grade dance held at the high school gym and it was something the school had done for years. Kinda like a prom for dads and their daughters to dress up at and a time for the daughters to see in their dads the kind of man he wished for her, and for her to seek the love in a man's heart that she could see in her dad's eyes.

Dads would get a special ring, present it to his daughter, and place it on her ring finger and lock that spot in hopes that they make a promise to each other that she treasure her body and her heart as much as her dad does and not allow a man to come between that promise unless he could show her he loved her as much as her dad did. It was a symbol of love and trust that was worn like a shield to remind her about the vow between her and her dad if she was ever in a position with a boy that was full of summer love or boyfriend romance. It was a ring that young girls talked about all through middle school, it was as sought after as much as a class ring was. It was a time that a dad would accept the talk of boys and boys calling the house to talk to his daughter. Looking back know, I can see that it was such a strong tradition because it may have made it easier for a dad to see his little princess grow up and it set the bar for dads of sons to raise their sons with respect so when the time was right they could seek the hand of a middle school sweetheart or approach that beautiful girl who gives him butterflies or makes him nervous when she is around.

Dads looked forward to raising boys the same as dads did raising daughters. It was a time that dads could see that they raised them to be young and decent men and it would show because those were the boys that were sought out. And those were the boys who were hired by the feed store and by the big sawmill and both were highly paid jobs for any high school boy who would want to go out on a Friday night or take a girl to a movie on a date. It was something that people in this town did over and over for years and it had families who moved here stay in this town because of its strong ties to family values. Families who were here stayed and families who heard of this would move here for that same benefit. And this was something my dad and I had both looked forward to my whole life. Not having a mom, my dad and I were already close but this was a time Dad could ease up on me and let me be more help to him and me. I could be left alone now, I could get an after-school job, and it was a time Dad could see I was getting older and all the time he had sacrificed on me he could get back for himself.

I remember of times I would ask my dad can I work, can I sleep over, can I stay out late, can I have a boyfriend, and always to every question was the same answer, 'wait till you're older, wait till the dance.' It was like a subtle way for him to say not yet without saying no. No was something my dad had trouble saying to me, not to say he wouldn't or he didn't because he said no a lot. It was just I could see he didn't like saying it, I already didn't have a mom and with him working and being gone so much, there were times he felt I was alone and I know that bothered him much. This was so special for my dad and me. We would go to our pizza place and get two large pizzas and a pitcher of drink and gorge out and talk of the day, we would dance my youth away. We would laugh and talk, only stopping for the occasional belch from the super loaded pizza and the pitcher of drink we were having. Oh the good old days where a dad could enjoy his princess showing her tomboy side before womanhood robbed her memory of how much fun dad was when he could belch louder and deeper than her and how a high five was like a first place trophy and replaced her memory with properness and manners.

He knew I would go from a girl who could burp her full name to a lady who would not be caught doing it at all, let alone in public, and the worse part about it was I didn't know until I was older just how important those moments were to him and just how much he was losing as a dad by me turning into a lady. He knew he was once a man who was my hero, he was once the strongest man I knew and he was the one who ruled over the box of tools that had the wrenches that could fix a bike, tighten a chain, or repair a hole in a tree house and turn into the man who I would want to drop me off outside places and not walk me in and be the man who I wouldn't share secrets with and who wouldn't have someone to play booger finger with anymore. I was gaining a lot and my dad was losing just as much. What kept him going was he kept trying to change with the time clock that was facing him every day the dance got closer.

I can appreciate the man he is by remembering the man he was. All of us in our little group were so excited, we spent every minute of our free time working on the plans at school and on our dresses.

We would look at all the dresses in every store window and in every new catalog that came out, trying to top the girls before us. Trying to be more beautiful than all the girls before us. We did more chores and more side jobs that summer than ever before. More yards got racked, cars were washed, and gutters were cleaned out on our street. The dance was in the middle of my ninth grade year, and I never knew until going through some of his old things that dad was waiting on that day since the day I was born. He had written me a letter every birthday of every year telling me how special I was and how exciting it was that year being my dad. He was secretly trying to lose some weight by never finishing junk food when we would eat out saying 'oh I'm full or oh I don't feel well' and while on work trips, he would eat healthy like a salad and something baked instead of pizza and a cold drink or something fried as we would do. He was also taking dancing lessons on nights I would have sleepovers or if a school project took up my evening. And tell me he was running errands.

I never really got to know just what all my dad went through and gave up for me let alone what he did for that dance. All I can do is wonder and appreciate what I knew he did because that was enough and that was what I did see him do and I love him dearly for that. We as young women, we gave our all and put it into that moment we would be free and never knew that growing up took so much out of the people who loved and raised us. Like I said, we shopped and shopped till our feet hurt. I had a white ball gown that was to some a little mature for my age but it was my night to be a woman and beside my dad I felt so safe and could be as beautiful as my imagination would allow me to be. Ohh how it sparkled, it was a one shoulder, thin strapped dress with diamonds across the waist, now I know by the price I got it for that it was no way near real diamonds but in that dress you could not tell me anything. (Gasping) It came tight down my waist showing what hips I did have and was cut just below the hipline exposing my whole right leg. And no dress is a dress no matter how awesome without a pair of matching heels and man I had them too.

They were six-inch heels with a strap that came across my ankle and slightly up my calf and then buckled. When those shoes touched my feet, I was a woman all the way through. My dad on the other hand wore suites for work and never dressed up when he was off the job, around the house it was gym shorts and tank tops and even for church it was pants and a dress shirt. I would say "Dad, really, its church, dress up," and I always got the same answer in that deep daddy voice, "Button, GOD knows my closet and last night when I prayed we discussed what to wear and I picked this out and he agreed so you wouldn't wanna question his fashion taste, would you?"

I would reply in the most hopeless expression and say, "Woooo, there is no dealing with you, you are like a big kid, I'm watching what I cannot correct. Even in a fuss he always seemed to make it fun and now looking back he never really made me feel like a child, I mean I know I was a kid but he never made me feel like a child. Oh how I miss that man!"

Chapter 3

The Wreck

It seemed everything in my life was coming together, school was going great, my friends were close and active in my life, and my dad and I were as close as we had ever been. With my mom being gone most of my life, I knew Dad was alone inside, I mean I knew he had me but the comfort of a companion is what he was missing and the girls and I had just the plan. There was a new manager at the store we all worked at who just moved into town, she was a fox. Just a year younger than Dad, she was never married, had long black hair and long legs, she was a kid like lady who fit right in with us. There were lots of times when it was easy to forget she was a grown lady outside the fact she was our boss (laughing). We would trick them in being at the same place at the same time to see them together. We would split up, me and Carla would take Dad to a movie while Kayle and Madison would take Miss Treasure and we would all meet up like it was just a rare act of events, then we would all pick a movie they wouldn't watch and take off, leaving them alone together.

We know it was a dirty trick, but it was a plan that worked a few times before they caught on or that was unless they caught on early and never led on to it. Because it was obvious they were into each other. When our movie would start we would sneak out of our movie and ease into theirs, with a little flirting from Madison and some brave fist balling from Kayle and we were in. Andy always had a soft spot for Madison so a few bats from the eyelashes would have him in a trance and he would not only let us swap movies but always seemed to have Madison a fresh drink on hand. So back to my point, we would sit in the back like shadows hoping to catch a hug, an arm reach, shared popcorn or anything. And we were sure to be very quiet not to be noticed. And it was a well-thought-out plan or so we thought. We went over every detail like steps on a ladder, careful not to leave out even the smallest of details. We really thought we had everything worked out. And then as fast as we had it, it all came unraveled. It seemed we covered everything but the one thing that got us busted (the reaction), yes the reaction, there was no planning for that moment.

Like a play from any playbook, Dad found his moment and moved in with a slight pass with his arm behind her neck resting it on her shoulder. And with a little effort on his part she rested her head on him, and like cheerleaders at a super bowl we were in the dark dancing with joy and everything was doing great until they took a long stare before leaning in for what would have been one of the most romantic kisses any woman could dream of. But it was cut short by the teenage scream from not one but four girls just five rows back who were screaming like they were at the front row of a boy band concert. My heart was racing like I was facing that fearful moment with my dad, and I couldn't hold back screaming, "GO DADDY! GO DADDY!" over and over like I was trying to lose my voice with every scream. Well it was safe to say that after a very embarrassing moment and a whole lot of explaining they never went to the movies with either of us again and seemed to be more suspicious of us all.

After we all laughed over it, some truth came out. It seemed the ones who knew it all weren't us at all, they had been on a few dates already and seemed to really be into eachother and that was far from their first kiss. We were so happy for them. Miss Treasure spent a lot of time with us and really enjoyed having a teenage girl in her life, like I said before she was a big kid still at heart and I had someone I could share the female side of life with. And it was so funny seeing the effects she had on my dad. She would come over and have supper and stay late and just so happen to be back over for breakfast, yea right. So the more she got close to us, the more we all relied on each other, when Dad was on the road she would sleepover so I was never alone. So that's why the night of the dance she was so important to Dad and I, he was already behind with his plane being held up by the weather, it was all Miss Treasure and I could do to stay calm. We had enough to keep us busy getting prettied up, both like two same age teens dressing for a night that would change our lives forever. Both loving the same man, both wanting to be in his life, and have him in our lives.

Yes that night would change our lives forever way more than we ever expected. With the call coming in finally from Dad's phone saying he had landed and for us to go on and go to the dance and he would meet us there. I only remember screaming, "I love you, Dad, and be careful…wooooo tonight I become a woman" and seeing the smile on her face when she said, "He said he loves you, button," and the look of happiness on her face as they said I love you to each other before hanging up. That would be the last time I see that look of peace and love on her face. It was long after that we were at the school and on the inside standing with Carla, Kayle, and Madison like we were at the red carpet of a fancy movie set. We were watching the door for him to walk in as each girl was escorted away to take her dance with her dad, and Miss Treasure and I was focusing on the music and trying not to worry. All at once the sound of sirens cut into the gym and drowned out the music as if fifty fire trucks were inside with us.

We found ourselves in a deep state of worry, not hearing that the music had stopped and we also didn't notice that one of the teachers that came late came in with such force that see jammed open the door making the sound of rescue traffic even louder, and the crowed spread open from the door straight to us. We were still looking at the fear on each other's faces, only thinking the worse and both knowing how alone we would be if we lost Dad. And I must have been totally out of it because I never felt the teacher take my hand nor did I see the tears falling from her face and my trance was only broken when the girls screamed, "OHHHH GOD! NOOOO!" The look on her face only said the worse about my dad. See she was late due to a fatal wreck at the main red light in town where a drunk driver hit my dad and both he and my dad were killed. The wreck was so horrific that the teacher told Treasure not to take me to the wreck and to take to the hospital instead. I lived the scariest night of my life that night. The loss of my mom was something I grew up with, but the loss of my dad was devastating.

The rest of the night was mainly a blur. It was spent at the hospital waiting room, although the doctors told us my dad had passed instantly and there was a strong chance due to the massive head trauma that his death was fast and that he didn't suffer. But the scare of that night would change our lives forever. Miss Treasure and I just sat holding each other and crying all night. Her losing her love of her life and me now both parents, we were both helpless and hopeless. I don't remember much of what got us through that night but I will never forget her telling me over and over that I wasn't alone and we had each other. I could only wonder how she must have felt trying to put the pieces of her own life together after her own heart was breaking, but looking down at a parentless teenager and having to put her own feelings and mourning aside to comfort me instead. I don't remember falling asleep but we both were awakened by the morning shift telling us that she had cold juice and hot coffee if we wanted. The poor lady must have thought we were rude as we just looked around and got up and walked out. I almost stopped and spoke to her when I saw a night shift nurse lean in and say they lost their husband and dad last night.

Sadness filled the room as every woman thought of her husband and dad as they tried to show their concern and tears filled the eyes of everyone who had seen us or heard what happened. The sadness was just them caring I know, but it was stealing the air from every breath we tried to take and we just wanted to get away. We went all the way home not saying a word, but somehow knowing that we would have each other. So it was not uncomfortable for me to see her make herself at home in my house. We both knew that we were just doing what we had to and we knew we would have to address our future soon and as of now we just wanted to comfort each other. What felt like days passed before we decided to get properly dressed, let alone leave the house. And it wasn't till the day the pizza could not be delivered and we were starving that we cleaned up and went to get lunch. We seemed to find a smile or two that day and it got easier as the days followed.

Chapter 4

The Finding of the Jacket

Like I said the days following were easier as they came with some hope that the pain of our loss would someday help our hearts heal. A few weeks after Dad's passing and the funeral, the courts allowed Miss Treasure to gain custody of me and she moved out of her apartment and moved into the house. And we agreed to set a plate for Dad every time we sat at the table. But after eating and looking at that plate just set there, we didn't have the heart to speak and we were so quiet that a simple meal was more miserable than a tribute to him, and if eating at that table wasn't bad enough we were not ready for when we were done. We both sat, we could not feel our feet for neither wanted to be the one to dump his plate. So we both just left it and went upstairs and cried ourselves to sleep. I didn't dream that night at all and was awakened at about ten A.M. to the sound of the dishwasher and I remembered Dad's plate. I flew out of bed, sliding down the stairs with my sock feet landing on the kitchen floor.

I knew I startled her as she spun around thinking I may have hurt myself. And like two eagles seeking their prey our eyes met, then we looked at the table at where Dad's plate was and to my surprise where I thought I would find a cold plate of food, I found a clean table and a flower setting in the middle of it. It was a very awkward moment and I saw the fear in her eyes as if she felt by changing things she may have done something wrong.

I didn't have the heart to make her feel bad after all we had been through, then all at once we burst out laughing and never really spoke of that moment and decided to eat in the living room after that. We both made a promise to make each other laugh at least once a day after that. Well, summer was upon us and it was time our days got longer as Treasure went back to work and the girls and I were back to our old cutting up. Mornings of junk food followed by sunning at our local pool to hours and hours of doing nothing, oh what a life. We forgot what happened to Dad's wrecked car as the days passed on and we never had a chance to see it up close anyway or at least that's what I thought.

It seems my three friends had not only seen it up close once but returned to see it as they missed my dad as much as I did for they grew up with him in their lives just as I had. So it must have brought them some closure because one day on the way home from the pool, they took me past the old wrecking yard where the car was stored. I did not know why the name on the sign looked familiar to me as I gazed at it as we got closer. With every step came a flash in my head as pictures shown over and over and like a camera out of focus they only came in clear as my memory came back to me. After seeing that sign on the door of the wrecker truck while I was passing a wreck that the police

29

had being cleaned up on the way to the hospital, it hit me, it was Dad's wreck as well. The closer we got, I could see the truck and I saw a gray mangled car under a tree with ribbons and flowers around it. With a heavy heart and weak knees, I managed to keep walking as the tears eased down my face, not a painful cry but one more of peace and acceptance.

Somehow in all that pain, I found some peace and we all stopped and looked through the fence and the girls told me everyone in town comes by to show their love.

They held me as we were all holding back the tears and they asked me was I okay and to my surprise I was. I was okay, I wanted to go inside so we did and at first we would just sit and stare at it and each of us would go over a funny moment or a happy memory we had with Dad. We went so often that the owner put up a wooden bench to give us a seat and get us off the ground. Time always seemed to stand still when we were there, I didn't realize that I was getting home so late and so often that Treasure began to worry so she followed us one day, not that she thought we were doing something wrong, she just knew as fussy as we were about being on time that she knew I must really be passionate about something and she wanted to be a part of it. And when she saw what it was, she didn't have the heart to intrude on our time so she never spoke of her knowing, she just found herself compelled to spend her lunch breaks sitting on that same bench looking at the same empty car we did over and over. And this went on for a while and no one knew that the other was there except Treasure, but the owner watched us as we all sat looking over.

We ran into the owner getting pizza one night and he pulled Treasure off to the side and explained to her that he knew about all of us coming to see the car and he told her the insurance company wanted the car and he had put them off for as long as he could but they were coming to get it. She knew that the news had to be hard to deliver but she could tell there was something else that he wasn't saying but she didn't push it. So she just asked if she and I could come say goodbye first and the man's voice muffled and his skin flushed like cold water was in his blood. He gathered every bit of strength he had and said, "Ma'am, don't you think that may be too much on her saying goodbye to the car her dad and boyfriend died in?" Shock came over her as she knew I didn't have a boyfriend and she was lost at how he could come up with that thought. He could tell that this news was puzzling to her and he explained (well the letterman jacket in the front is her boyfriend's). She asked him to let her in before the car was taken and not to speak of the jacket to anyone and they both went away. When I made it back to the car, I could see the wonder in Treasure's face.

The whole ride home was quiet, not like a 'I'm mad you did something wrong' quiet. I just passed it off as the man must have brought my dad up and she needed some time so I didn't make a fuss over the silence. She was still quiet most of the night, breaking her silence only to answer me but not to carry the conversation, just a word or two in response and that was it. The next day, she was at the gate when the owner opened it and she ran to the car, climbing into the wreckage as fast as someone would be fast getting out of the wreckage (with a chuckle). I would

31

have given anything to see her rip into that car looking for the jacket he spoke of. And with some help from tools and the owner's forklift she managed to free the jacket without a scratch.

She cleaned up and went to work waiting to get off to share this info with me. Not knowing how the jacket got there and not being from around there, she didn't have any idea what school it was from or who it could be for. The thoughts must have been more than she could bear because she found herself researching that night, calling the cops and asking questions, spending her whole lunch break talking to witnesses over and over.

After days of asking around and checking into the story of that horrible night over and over with the witnesses and all telling the same thing about a young man being seen running from his car to my dad's car then running from the wreck never to be seen again. She was torn between not telling me about the mysterious jacket and reliving the pain of that night as each story was told with clear and vivid details. I cannot imagine the heartache she put herself through just to get to the bottom of the stranger but she just couldn't live without knowing what really happened. And wondering if that kid could have done something to save the love of her life or was something he did that took his life. And either way she was compelled to seek out the truth. Several days had come and gone with Treasure looking into the wreck and with little to go on and not knowing any more than there was someone else there who knew just a bit more than everyone else, just more than she could bear. When she was certain she had gone as far as she could on her own, and she had met with everyone explaining what she had found. She knew that what she found would change everything about that horrible night and it was a major key in that wreck, and she knew that it was time to tell me.

So she asked me to come in as soon as she got off work one day, out of the blue, I didn't think much of it but all that changed once I met her at the door, me holding a bag of chips and her holding a jocks letterman jacket having the school colors I had never seen before. The look on her face was that of no sleep and worry. But I could see the confusion of wanting to tell me something but not knowing where to start and not knowing how I would react. So after a brief silence, I asked, "Who's the jacket for, and why did you need me?"

As soft as a mother reading a bedtime story to a sleepy baby, she softly replied, "Come, we need to talk." She took a deep breath and began, she explained from the start. From finding out we were visiting Dad's car to why the tow truck owner wanted to talk and where and how she found the jacket. Sure it was hard not to butt in and ask a thousand questions but I was at the edge of my chair hanging on to every word. For every time she said something, it was more important than before.

No matter how many questions I had or even tried to ask, not any one of them could have been as important as what she was saying. She explained the details of each witness who had all seen the same guy doing the same thing; leaving the car that hit Dad with a heavy jacket on and then moments later running from Dad's car with just a tee shirt on. Which left me instantly with the same thought Treasure had. What did he know, what did he see, could he have helped or could he have taken my dad's life. Either way, these were questions that we just couldn't leave unanswered.

So we started with the jacket, we looked for names on the inside and we only saw (HAMMER), we knew that had to be a nickname and the football patches showed he was a seasoned player but the school colors were way too flashy for our small town. With little help from the local police and little help from the town, we were seeing our dream of finding out anything slowly slipping away. The local police called it an open-and-shut-case of DWI where two men lost their lives, end of story. And when we brought up the jacket and the sighting of a stranger, they all said the same thing, find him and we will question him, until then we have nothing, and as far as the jacket was concerned, they said it had no reflection on the cause of the crash.

Everywhere we turned after that showed us just how past the wreck the town had become. The town that stuck together while I was a child seemed to just become cold and emotionless. We asked so many people and bothered so many people that even going to town was getting harder for us, from being stared at to being avoided, it was clear we were the crazy ladies in town. Except for my girls, they had my back and thank GOD for that because over the next year I was really gonna need them, in a big way we would need each other.

After it was clear we weren't getting anywhere on our own, Treasure decided to put the jacket in the closet and told us to take some time and let things settle down. She returned to her daily routine work and gym, and I wanted to help her normalize her life as much as I could, so the girls and I never spoke of the wreck, Dad, or the jacket in front of her. But I knew acting normal wasn't gonna hold up because her heart was hurt too bad, she grieved and was so lonely she would sleep in Dad's old shirts and I would catch her looking at the jacket hoping for a clue to what happened that night.

Chapter 5

Another Loss

We both had hurt so much that I tried to be strong for me and her. I would run to town for her and I would leave the house for her and I guess I never saw that the more I helped her, the more shut away she became. Soon she turned into a ghost in her own life, she just went to work and home. The gym stopped, the walks in the park stopped, hair pulled up instead of fixed, then little makeup went to no makeup at all. I never realized she was slipping away as I became more involved in school. The group and I were balancing out and the more Treasure's life was falling apart, my life was finally coming together. When you promise someone you will always be there for them you never really know the depth to that promise. We made that promise and it wasn't till it was too late that we saw we failed at that promise. When you love someone and you see them slipping away from the normal and you don't step in and help them get back on track, it's that moment then that you failed them.

Watching them act out of character and you going on in your own life as if nothing is wrong only makes them feel more normal in the chaos that has taken over their life. If I would have known my acting normal contributed to Treasure's downfall I would have stepped in long before it got so bad. People deal with the loss of a love one in their own way and I lost two parents so that loss is hard but I could not imagine the loss of a boyfriend or husband because days turned into months and her health deteriorated so fast that I had never realized she was hurting by being alone and missing Dad. I never thought anything of it when the girls dropped me off from school that evening, seeing Treasure's SUV home that early wasn't a surprise so I grabbed the door, not even reaching for my key, thinking with her being home the door would be opened. But I felt the door was locked as I had left it that morning. I dropped my stuff in the little chair as I walked in, emptied my arm, and called for Treasure in a loud voice. Only paused to hear the noise coming from her room, not knowing if it was music or her alarm clock, it was so loud it was clear she would not hear me so I ran upstairs calling her name over and over.

I reached the top and realized she had not left the house, her uniform still lay on the handrail of the upstairs ledge, at that time I felt something may be wrong... I pushed open her door, hoping to find her gorging some ice cream, the depressed woman's go to food. I was not ready for what I saw, the woman who was my best friend, laying there lifeless. The girls must not have had ample time to leave because when I screamed they stopped and ran through the door I left open. They found me on the floor, Treasure lay over her bed lifeless with one hand holding a pitcher of her, Dad, and I, and the other slightly open with a half empty bottle of sleeping pills. The pale, cold skin on her face was an indication that she had taken her own life. I had now lost three parents and I was lost and confused. I don't know much about that day but I know I never wanted to end up like that. When the girls finally got me up, I stood over her as we all cried, and I asked my friends right then to never let me get that bad, to please step in, to please never look into my eyes and see nothing and not do something.

We called the police and they came, took our statements, and properly removed the body. Carla's mom showed up and had me gather some things and move to their home as being there alone at my age wouldn't be a good idea after all I'd been through. So we locked up the house, and I tried to put these days behind me. After losing another loved one, I realized my heart had been through more than I was ready for, although I didn't know then how connected to my dad's wreck all this was and how that night changed my life forever. The house was a home Dad paid off early in life and he had an insurance policy that Treasure set up for me before she decided to leave this earth. So I was well taken care of on the money side of things but outside our group I didn't get attach to others and did not let anyone in either. I would go by from time to time as the school year came to an end. The long summer days allowed for us to go inside the house and pack up Treasure's things, she never had kids so we kept her stuff in the attic with Dad's stuff, we felt that was best. We found it to be easier than we thought it was until we came across it.

It was the letterman jacket that sent her on a search that broke what little heart she had left. It took the very last breath from her, killed her, and left her without any of the answers she sought. I stared at it, almost too scared to touch it, fearing it had some kinda power to take lives. Although any other day that would sound crazy but today I was standing in the house of my dead father where that jacket had been found in his wrecked car and now I was standing in the closet of the room where Treasure took her own life looking at the same jacket; so this day was not normal on any scale. Kayle being the bravest of us all quietly spoke and coming from someone as loud as she was it's funny how we listened to her more when she spoke softly than when she was loud. She said, "Y'all take her downstairs, I'll remove the jacket and take it to the attic." That's what they did and we locked up and left. Not being around that jacket and not seeing Dad's car under that same oak tree at the wrecking yard downtown, I found my life having hope to level off. I put my mind on school and being an animal vet and only looked ahead not behind me. Our plans were to open a vet's office and work together once we were outta high school.

Normal in a word has a clear meaning but normal in definition is all in interpretation. When you live in chaos then what is normal? Not having a mom I never really knew what I was missing by only being raised by my dad. When my dad passed, I finally had a mother figure without a dad. Normal was something I stopped looking for and tried to just make it through the day and leave yesterday alone in hopes that in my days I could look forward to my week ahead till that turned into months. That kept me stable, I was too broken to find normal. I had money in the bank, a roof over my head, and a plan; that's all I had time for. We all took jobs that would help us with our hopes of our own vet's office and we studied every chance we got. The other three girls in our group had relationships and they were patient with me and didn't make me feel bad because I didn't share their need for a companion. Love to me meant loss and I had lost enough to love, nope, love wasn't for me and they knew that. Besides, I don't know if I was bitter or boys found me to be bad luck because I wasn't asked to go out by anyone anyway.

Chapter 6

Hello from the Past

I was far from being a cat lady, I was tall and beautiful, I just had no trust in love, and I guess boys picked up on that and no matter how amazing you look, not believing in love has to be ugly in every sense. Graduation was a few months away and we all were sure to pass. We had our senior trip all planned out, it was ocean view and sand in our toes and sun on our skin. Carla's family really stepped in for me. The last years of school were easier, being stable and being in a house full of people made not feeling lonely easy. It was always noisy with her brothers bothering us and her parents always had family and friends over to swim and cook out. It was easy to be numb to my own sadness when I could live as someone else in their family. Soon graduation came and the after party at the big hall was where we all went to celebrate. It was a fun night with plenty of friends to send us off. Everyone knew everyone except that one older guy who was as much the star as we were due to the fact that he was new and in whispered voices people were asking who he was and where did he come from.

The only time I could ever say I really have seen him was behind the old tire shop in town. I always thought he was homeless. I wondered if he had a child he was there to see and how someone who had grown up like me without a parent, only to find out years later that they had a dad. I was correct about the part that he was here to see someone and I came to know exactly who as he approached me, grabbed my hand, and with a wheezy old man's voice, he asked me if he could have a minute. Without knowing what on earth he could have to talk to me about and my curiosity getting the best of me, I agreed. He was so old and bent over from bad living conditions that I felt I should be helping him as we walked, but he firmly gripped my right arm and pulled himself together and escorted me as the lady he saw me as. He found a bench outside the hall under a low burning streetlight as if to hide, I guess from years and years of being alone and hiding in a weird way I could relate and I too felt okay being in the dim light. He took my hand and said, "Dear, for many moons I've watched you and wanted to know if you got his message," and at this time I started thinking he was just an old man who was scaring me.

He kept telling me he knew my dad tried to send me a message. The old man could tell I was getting upset and he must have been torn between just walking away or finishing, and with his age and poor health he pushed on to ask me to hear him out. He added that he knew Treasure got the jacket and he thought then the message was gonna come out but the loss was too much for her and he did not want the same to happen to me. He spoke of her with such passion that it was as if he knew her as I would find out

42

later that he was her dad and he had a good job and it was only when Treasure was a baby that her mom left him and took her and moved away and refused to let him see her. He fell into deep depression, lost his job, then his house, and gave up so he made his home behind the old tire station and watched over it at night. He was there the night my dad was hit, he told a story that shook me from the inside. He said when Dad's car was hit, the driver of the other car died instantly. But your dad was screaming help me, my heart stopped, could he be right, why hasn't he told the cops, he went on to say he heard Dad scream as the passenger got out hollering I'm not going to jail. He said a passenger, meaning there was someone else there.

Not only was someone else there but they knew what had happened to my dad. With a face full of tears I was hanging on to every word. He said the kid had a big jacket on and was screaming, "Shut up, dude, die already!" He approached the passenger side of Dad's car and saw Dad was alive, he pulled open the door and saw me standing there asking him to help my dad. The kid pushed me away and told me to go back where I came from and said he wasn't leaving any witnesses. He said if I didn't wanna die with this guy then I should leave and stay quiet. Your dad with his last bit of life fought to the very end. He whipped his bloody face then grabbed the kid's arm to show he was there when all at once the kid grabbed a piece of broken metal and smashed Dad in the face until he was no longer breathing. Then he wiped his sleeve clean through his jacket and said the truth dies with you old man. He touched my head as he looked away and said, "You must think I'm a coward, don't you?"

43

I hugged him saying, "No, I do not, sir, there was nothing you could have done. Don't blame yourself at all." He went on to say he used a handheld type radio and hid in some bushes and after the wreck was cleared out, a cop car picked him up, and they left.

I thought my life could not get more complicated from the loss of my family to the never-ending drama and now I find out that Dad may have lived and was killed not by just a kid but a kid who was hauled away by a cop. The old man told his story just as he lived it that night and every night after in his nightmares. He walked the streets every night scared to fall asleep because he heard Dad's voice in his head over and over. He told me he was drunk every day since that day until he saw my face in the paper and he knew I would be here so he sobered up and came to tell me that my dad fought for his life and I needed to seek the jacket out and find the man who killed my dad. The old man saw the crowd that was watching me cry and he wished me good luck and vanished into the darkness of the night. My sobbing was interrupted by the presence of my three sister-like best friends holding me as I cried as I had many times before. In a panic there was no way I could ever get out what had happened between me and the old man as he opened up to me. As Carla was hanging her car keys over her shoulder, I knew my dad's house key was on that ring so I leapt up, snatching them up, and running to her car as a trail of girls followed behind me.

I unlocked the driver's door and gave just a brief minute for them to get in as I drove away. I sped away going as fast as I could, nearing my house with every mile, hearing them asking me where we are going and hanging

44

on for dear life. We pulled up at my house and I killed the car and ran to the door, unlocked it and was halfway up the stairs before the girls caught up to me. I busted into the room across the stairs where Treasure took her last breath, they stood at the door as I dug in the closet like I lost a winning lottery ticket. Knowing this room and my history and my panicked state of mind, it was obvious to Kayle what I was looking for and she knew I wasn't going to find it there as she remembered on that horrible night that she took the jacket and brought it to the attic to store it. Like a disappearing shadow when a light comes on, she slipped out of the room. That's when she knew it was time to go to the attic and get the jacket. It wasn't long and she returned with a strange high school looking jacket while we were sitting in the living room on the long couch where we had been waiting. After I went front to back, left to right, and top to bottom what felt like a thousand times, the other two jumped in and started looking and without trying to be funny asked, "What are we looking for?"

I was exhausted and out of breath when I fell back on the bed, holding my head saying over and over, "It's not here, it's not here," and Madison being Madison always found the strangest things to say, at what always seemed to be at the wrong time but always worked out for us.

She said, "Talk about doing this over again, the last time we were in here like this…Kayle walked out…" Then like a light went off in Carla's head, she grabbed my hand, and pulled me downstairs, dragged me as fast as she could, as we both went sliding down the last step, falling at the feet of Kayle holding the jacket I looked so hard for.

She had it lying across her lap and asked only one question, "What happened tonight that caused us to enter this nightmare all over again?" I explained from start to finish, word to word what the old man had shared with me on that park bench just a few hours ago. I told them the story of how my father lost his life at the hand of a thug who killed him. And that jacket held the key my dad sent me to tell me what happened. I told them that the old man was Treasure's dad and he was homeless and we had to do something for him.

With our thoughts in a whirlwind and all of this happening at once we had no idea where to start so we jumped in the car and went to the old tire shop, hoping to find the nameless man who had impacted my life with all the answers that Treasure took her life over because she couldn't find them. We honked and screamed until he came out thinking something was wrong or he was in trouble and he knew with age and the stress being homeless had put on his body and mind that he was in no shape to harm us. We calmed down long enough to tell him we were not there to get him in trouble but we were there to offer him a home and a family and we would start with a shower and a hot meal. We loaded him up and brought him to my house and gave him a room and his own bathroom, it was a life he could only dream about. It was a few months before we gathered our thoughts together on how to handle the news that had come to us by the wonderful old man who was found to be named Douglas Gray. The man who was just a body in a back of a tire shop only seen by the nighttime sky now had a name and a home with four new granddaughters.

Over the next few weeks, we managed to gather some of his things from his little shack, it was some weathered covers, some old pitchers, and some metals from his days in the military. It was not easy talking him into letting go of some old clothes as it was one of the only few things he had ever truly owned. But with some persuading we gathered him up and spent our free time helping him adjust to his new life so he could spend the rest of his life in comfort as he deserved. We all had a new grandpa and we all had a blast settling him in and visiting him, vowing to not let him feel alone ever again. It was funny as he learned how to use a microwave or a washer and dryer, and when he came up missing we could always find him in the grade tub upstairs, it was his hot tub and his thinking space (laughing). Yes, it was a long overdue gift having him in our life as we were a blessing in his life.

Chapter 7

The Plan

After settling in our new grandfather figure, we took some time for ourselves. I could not get away from the thought of my dad sending me a message from his last moments alive while fighting for his life. I was filled with so many emotions ranging from hate to revenge that every breath I took was only fueling my life to hunt down the man who took my father's life and make him pay with his own life. Now I know an eye for an eye is only an expression but that phrase was the only thing that brought me peace of mind. I tossed around many different ideas to hunt him down and every one ended the same way, they all had the same problem. I could not do it alone. Now I knew I had friends who were like birth sisters to me, we had already proven to have each other's back in life. We had been through so much more than most people our age and knowing that, how could I ask them to give up any more of their lives for me.

It was clear what I had to do without dragging them into any more of the drama that was my life. I had it all planed out, I would get them over and let them know I was gonna go away for a while and I wanted to hang out before I took some time for myself. After all I had been through and being out of school now, it was a very believable plan and I knew they would understand that I could use some time to get away. Or at least that was where my intentions were headed. With money in the bank and Douglas taking care of the house I was going through with this no matter what. I spent the next few days contacting the girls, asking them for a dinner date at my house for some us time and that I had some news to share with them. With the weekend approaching my plan was coming together, it seemed for once in my life I was focused and I knew clearly what I wanted and was brave enough to go get it. I never stopped to ask was it bravery or rage, but either way it was enough to make me feel alive, or I was numb to the pain of my past. But just when I thought everything was coming together, that simple old man that I had in my house started talking to me like he had lost his mind or like he thought I had lost mine. His words were more of a professor in a college room talking to scholars or a military man about to take his men into battle but either way it was not the man I thought I knew when he was just a broken and humble man of age who could barely carry himself. And now he was talking with deep thought and conviction as if he was getting me ready for battle as if he could see into me and already knew my intentions. The remarks said low as he passed were phrases directed to me and just as fast as I heard them and took them in stride he had moved by, and I found myself left with the message he sent with no way to respond. From 'walk fast and think slow, for only when the mind wanders is when you make mistakes' to 'eyes are the windows to the soul, be careful who you look at or your secret will expose you' and 'before you enter a journey of trouble, educate your mind for battle.'

It was as if he could look into my soul and see the revenge I was after. I tried to put aside the fact that he noticed my actions and focus on the plan at hand. Besides, with his wisdom I wasn't gonna act like he didn't know what he was talking about, I just knew with his age he couldn't be much help. My phone rang off the hook that day with my girlfriends one after another chatting and talking like we did when we were younger. I was hoping that I wasn't as easy to read for them as I was to Douglas. I spent all day in the kitchen cooking our favorite meal. It was the first meal my dad taught us to cook. I can remember him now saying spaghetti is not a spaghetti without a great sauce and that don't come out of a can or jar. Dad would spend all morning cutting fresh bell peppers, onions, and tomatoes, cook ground meat until done, then drain fast to get some of the grease off the meat without letting the taste slip away. When mixed together and slow cooked for hours made the whole house smell like a walk through Italy on a warm sunny day. This dinner was supposed to be me talking to them about me going on an adventure. More of a 'wish me well, Im'a be okay' moment.

Backing away from the stove, a glass of wine in hand, looking over the awesome meal I fixed, before I could finish my first sigh, there came Douglas with his nonsense. He said, "They gonna see right through you, you should just tell them you going hunting." And as fast as he came in the kitchen like an eagle coming in to catch his prey, he spoke his mind then was gone, and all that was left was the empty thought echoing in my head over and over. *How would he know, what would he know, and am I that transparent because if I am and I can't hide this from a man I just met how will I ever keep this from the people I've known my whole life.* The sound of the front door opening and the loud voices from the three women who knew my every secret coming over took the sound of my own voice and froze me in place. I had never been so scared to be around them, ever, but the last thought going through my head left me with the fearful reality that they may find out before I tell them and they may not understand. That alone would devastate me. To my surprise the smell of dinner had overtaken the whole house and managed to distract them.

Conversation at the table was just as I had hoped, lots of laughter and memories, one story after another. It was almost too perfect. The laughing and joking was only interrupted by the presence of Douglas clearing his throat as he stared at me like he knew what was this dinner set up for. After avoiding him as much as I could, Kayle being as clever as she is spoke up, "Okay, is anyone gonna tell me why we are really here and why Douglas knows before we do, so either spill it or give him a throat drop." I gathered myself and started from the top, I told them everything without interruption. Not one mutter, not one squinted eye of disapproval, just a casual sip of drink to keep the throat wet and they gave their full attention to my every detail. I told my story, not leaving out a single thing. The silence made it easy for me, even the occasional nod from

51

Douglas was warming. After the plan was laid out in front of them, even the bitter talk of revenge was all out in the open, I sat there waiting for the vote of support from the only family I had left.

I was relaxed to have it off my chest finally and thought I was free, then I waited for their reaction, and all eyes were on me. With a few sips of wine and a few looks from across the room, Kayle moved slowly into the kitchen and opened the icebox. The eyes off me, I'm not gonna lie, was refreshing. She grabbed two beers, handed one to Douglas, snapped hers on the edge of the table, took a long swallow standing over her chair before spinning it around, and setting it backwards, then spoke like I never heard her speak before. She said, "Well, what's the plan on hunting this creep down and evening the score?" The reaction from us was loud as we all jumped up, all sharing the same thought as we loved my dad and had lost enough that night and we knew what we wanted to do. The next few weeks we planned every detail, not missing anything. Douglas took us like his own squad going into battle and we were ready for war.

Chapter 8

Plan in Motion

With Douglas coaching us and under his strict guidance, he trained us to think strong on the inside and out. You would think homeless people wouldn't have much, at least that's what I thought. With a few trips to the tire shop and a few more places, Douglas rounded up some more men and they came together like a group. They brought us to a field and had weapons and back stops and targets; it was the real deal. Now three of us felt like a duck out of water, never shooting a gun at all, but Kayle jumped out hollering, "Hell, yea, let's shoot some stuff!" I don't know how many rounds we went through but we went from shooting the tops of trees and rocks off the ground, by the time we were done, we could pierce the ear of a hummingbird with one shot. Now shooting a target was easy but killing a man we knew wouldn't be. I don't ever think we wanted to go there to kill him, we just wanted to be able to defend ourselves if it came to that. Enough of people have died already, I wanted the dying to stop, I just wanted the pain in my heart to go away, and I just wanted justice. It's just at that time I didn't know what that meant, I was hoping that would come to me soon.

The next few weeks were busy, we spent our Fridays at every adjoining town outside our city's limits looking for school colors to match the letterman jacket. We spent several weekends looking over and were about to give up when Madison's bladder spoke up. She couldn't ride in a car slamming cold drinks without having to pee every few minutes. Her bladder hit while we were on the highway and the only spot to stop was a little truck stop that looked far away to a woman with a small bladder. We all laughed as she was scared she had peed on herself. As we pulled in, she grabbed the letterman jacket instead of hers, putting it on as she ran to the bathroom, pushing through the truckers on her way. We all sat in the car about to give up as time seemed to stand still. The walk back must have been awkward for her as the man behind her looked like a linebacker and a biker had a son. He was a rough mountain of a man, the finger on the lip from Madison was our code for follow my lead so we were speechless until she spoke first.

She made it to the car and said, "Hey, girls, meet Tom, he knows Hammer." We hid our shock of not knowing anything and replied calmly. Then with a pull on the jacket we saw she had on the wrong jacket and she said he knew him, he played football against him at Morehead High just 30 miles from here. We snapped a story of romance and told Tom that we were trying to find him and we lost contact after a wild night and we wanna return his jacket. Yes, that's a far cry from the truth that we really wanted to blow his brains out and watch him bleed out. After the swap of a few lies and some flirting, we got all we needed to know and were off. We went back to the house and told Douglas everything, then spent the rest of the week taking time to clear our heads and focus on our job—revenge.

Chapter 9

The Call for Redemption

That next Friday came faster than I thought it would, but we were so ready and well trained that we just reacted like we were following a playbook. We rode around the town going from place to place looking for a guy who may not even live there anymore, all we had was a letterman jacket and a nickname. None of us had any idea of what he even looked like, until we walked into a little hamburger shop and we saw not only a pitcher of the guy we were looking for but a shrine of his last four years of high school football seasons. It was clear if he was anywhere in this town, finding him would be easy. He had pitchers and trophies all in this place as if this was the main stop after every game because this town loved their star quarterback. It didn't take long before the old lady behind the counter recognized the jacket on Madison's back, and the plan was in motion. We explained she was a special friend and it was easy to play a girl of his as everyone knows a guy that well known would have plenty. We went on to ask where a girl could meet him to return his jacket.

She was more than willing to contact him and sent us to a dirt road on the edge of town to meet. We rode on that dirt road, not saying a word. I told the girls if they wanted out to drop me off and leave, there was no reason for them to be dragged any further into this than they already were. With one look around, they said from start to finish we will be together and there was no way they wanted out. It was late already when we drove up and the sun was going down which cooled off the heat of the day but made visibility harder. A thousand thoughts came and went, what if he is not alone, what if we panic, just what ifs over and over. Then we remembered what Douglas taught us, breathe more and think less. Right when we thought we were wasting our time and it was time to just drive away, a truck's headlights could be seen in the dark of night and a huge 4x4 truck slid up about 50 feet from us. A tall, well-built man climbed out and with the headlights crossed, it was clear he could not see us. What happened next was not rehearsed and no amount of planning could have prepared us.

He was out the truck hollering, "Hello, you called for me." Everyone could see I froze up, neither had seen the other, so without a pause Kayle snatched the jacket, jumped out, and said, "Hammer, it's me." And knowing he could not see us, we eased out of the car, making sure we stayed in the darkness and out of the light. Kayle walked closer to him and the closer she got, the more nervous we got. Everything was going smoothly at first then everything went blurry. When she got close enough for him to see the jacket, we had no idea how violent it was about to get, even knowing how tough Kayle was, he was a very big guy. He grabbed her and moved her out of the light and with one punch forced her back, hit her head on his bumper, and knocked her out cold. We never got to see his face as he pulled the jacket off her limp body as she lay in the dirt, and he looked it over, reading his name inside the collar took him back to the very night he had been running from all these years. When one of us slipped in the loose gravel, he knew they were not alone and moved into the light, calling out to us.

Madison and Carla were already in the light and were worried about me so they spoke up and said, "We are here, it's us." He screamed, asking where did we get the jacket and who were we and was getting louder and scarier each time. Being a man and an athlete, he moved toward them, gaining on them before they had a chance to react. I ran to the car where I knew we had the pistol and saw the short space between the driver's seat and the door so I grabbed it. When I turned around, I saw my three friends taking the beating they did not deserve. He had one by the throat and the other by the head of the hair and Kayle was lying on the ground, not moving.

The thought of her being the toughest of us all and still going down first never crossed my mind and I was pissed like never before. I hollered, "Hey, buddy, I came for you, let them go, it's me you want." I moved into his sight and with a friend in each hand, being way smaller than either of them, he did not show any fear of me at all. The pistol pressed against my back and the smooth grip on the bar gave me the assurance I needed to hurt him or die trying.

The words he spoke were not heard by me as I swung the bar across his arm, almost breaking it as he let Carla go. Another swing to his leg and he dropped to his side, falling on Madison, then he caught the bar pushing me back while punching both the girls. While walking to his truck, Kayle spun and kicked him, stunning him only for a second before he threw her into a wooden fence. I felt the pistol in my back and without another thought I pulled it and fired a shot, stopping him from getting in the truck. I explained with another shot by his legs that he took something from me, then shot again, he never spoke as he counted every missed shot; not to thank GOD for the miss but waiting to have his chance to stop me. I listened to every shot trying to stay safe, waiting and hoping I would not be hit and kept this up till the gun clicked, showing it was empty. The man said, "Woman, you missed every shot and now ima kill you like I killed that crazy old man on that rainy night, ima smash your face in like I did that old man while he begged for his life."

Now holding an empty gun and hearing those hateful and hurtful words on any other day would probably be the end of me, but not the me who attended the Douglas class of self-defense: page one, give your opponent the false sense of winning. So with an empty gun he charged and with a slide of the left hand I took my spare clip, dropped the empty clip, reloaded faster than he would notice and the next shot was center mass in his chest. He dropped at my feet, the leverage the girls needed to regain their composure. They stood by me as I looked down at the man Treasure died trying to find and I had him. I asked him to say he was sorry and it would stop and he replied, "Never!" He grabbed a knife from his side and as he swung it, three more shots went off from my gun, ending

59

his life. He fell back with the force from the bullets stopping him. As we stood over his dead body, we paused for a moment before Kayle threw the jacket over him saying here's your jacket. And like that it was over, on that old gravel road, it was over. As we walked back to the car holding hands, it began to rain, wetting our faces, washing away our tears, and all the cries of our innocence.

Maintenance of Locomotive Boilers

Maintenance of
Locomotive Boilers

Edited by Allan Garraway

Ian Allan
PUBLISHING

Front cover: The sectioned boiler of Southern Railway 'Merchant Navy' class Pacific No 35029 *Ellerman Lines* as displayed at the National Railway Museum. *Ian Allan Library*

Rear cover, top: The chassis of Paris, Lyons Midi locomotive No 141C623 following a boiler explosion (see page 17). The driver and fireman were killed.

Rear cover, bottom: The main components of a locomotive boiler.

Front endpaper: With a maximum effort required for performance like this of No 5305 over Currour summit boiler standards must be high. *Moira Dalglish*

Title page: BR Standard Class 4MT hauls a steam powered breakdown crane along the East Lancs Railway. Another, often forgotten, example of a boiler requiring maintenance. *John Shuttleworth*

Frontispiece: John Bunch lights the fire in his Southern Railway 'N' class locomotive. This was the first time the locomotive had been steamed following initial restoration. The boiler currently awaits a further overhaul. *Mid-Hants Railway*

Back endpaper: Former industrial and American-built tank engines haul a train on the Kent & East Sussex Railway. Alternative approaches to get the same result, as different designs of locomotives require varying firing techniques, and driving techniques. One item remains the same however, the boilers require the same amount of time and effort on their maintenance. *R. Bamerough*

First published 1999

ISBN 0 7110 2746 3

Published by Ian Allan Publishing

An imprint of Ian Allan Publishing Ltd, Terminal House, Shepperton, Surrey TW17 8AS.

Printed by Ian Allan Printing Ltd, Riverdene Business Park, Hersham, Surrey KT12 4RG.

Code: 9910/A

CONTENTS

FOREWORD

The boiler is probably the most difficult part of a steam locomotive to maintain, with surprisingly very little having been written about this subject in the past, and the last generation of men, who regularly earned their living building and maintaining locomotive boilers is dwindling, together with the loss of knowledge and expertise.

Allan Garraway is one of the few people who has the ability to collect this past knowledge and experience and set it down on paper. He is well known in the Heritage Railway Association, and is an engineer with considerable general management experience. He has worked on both standard and narrow gauge railways and made a life study of steam locomotives.

For anybody dealing with locomotive boilers for the first time this is ideal reading. They will learn a lot. And for those more experienced it is an excellent reminder of the hazards and easily made costly mistakes. Allan rightly emphasises the need to record procedures, history and the work carried out. Only the correct standard of work is acceptable. With over 1,500 locomotive boilers in being, their care is of paramount importance and already too many failures and accidents have occurred. This book should help to reduce these in the future.

This introduction to locomotive boilers will, I am sure, be most useful to boilersmiths, insurance inspectors, footplate staff, engineers, general managers and those who are just interested in locomotives. Allan will not mind me saying that this is only an introduction, for there is much more to be said and learnt. Hopefully, this book will be the foundation for future specialised books and papers.

Finally, whilst this book is predominantly about older locomotive boilers, Allan also draws attention to the requirements for new boilers. He rightly emphasises that new ideas and techniques must be fully thought out and introduced in a controlled way.

I have enjoyed reading the book and it has reminded me of many important aspects of steam locomotive boiler maintenance and construction.

J. G. Butt, C.Eng.FIMechE
East Horsley, 1999

5

INTRODUCTION

Following discussions on the problems arising from some boiler inspectors having limited experience of loco type boilers, I was asked to write a small book on loco boilers and their maintenance.

The design of modern loco boilers would provide enough material for a large book, and was not what I felt was wanted. My main remit was to try to pick the brains of some of the few remaining people who had worked with steam locomotive boiler repairs and to try to put down some of their experiences before it was too late.

The days of steam locomotives in daily use for maintaining main line train services are almost forgotten. Today, steam locomotives are working tourist trains of one sort or another, in many cases operated and maintained by enthusiastic railwaymen in their spare time.

I have regarded myself as editor-in-chief to gather this information together; suffice it to say that a lot of people have made considerable contributions in the way of suggestions and points I had omitted, and to them I am extremely grateful, as without their input there would have been limited value in this book. Not everyone agrees with everything that we have written, it would have been strange if they had as there are more ways than one of repairing boilers, as with most engineering. Lastly, I must acknowledge Margaret Crane, for her work in typing up the drafts and continually amending them, as further comments and suggestions have come in.

A.G.W. Garraway
Vice President, Heritage Railway Association

The aftermath of the Buxton boiler explosion, 11 November 1921 (see page 16). *Ian Allan Library*

1 Locomotive-type Boilers: an Outline of First Principles

Grandmothers who already know how to suck eggs may omit this chapter, but there are those who may find it useful to have a few basic principles clarified. Please keep the following facts in mind.

Raising water to boiling point requires quite a lot of heat: turning water into steam needs a lot more. Consider how long it takes to boil a kettle and how much longer it takes to boil it dry. But there is one thing more to note: the boiling point of water varies according to the surrounding air (or steam) pressure: as pressure rises, so does the temperature of the boiling point. A consequence of this is that if steam at the same temperature and pressure as the boiling water it

came from is allowed to expand, its pressure reduces and it starts to condense back into water droplets. But if the steam is heated again beyond the temperature of the boiling water it came from, it is turned from 'saturated' into 'super-heated' steam, and can then expand a great deal — ie do useful work — before it starts to condense and lose pressure.

Practically everything expands when its temperature rises, but not everything expands at the same rate. Some metals, for instance, expand (and contract) much more than others over the same temperature change. Again, not all parts of a boiler are always at the same temperature: the firebox in a locomotive boiler will expand first

The sectioned boiler of Southern Railway 'Merchant Navy' class Pacific No 35029 *Ellerman Lines* as displayed at the National Railway Museum.

when the fire is lit, then the tubes, but the outside shell of the boiler will be at the same temperature as the water and heat up more slowly. Inevitably this will produce stresses and strains in the boiler, which unless they are allowed for in its construction will produce problems.

Water itself can present difficulties. These are minimised in ship and power station boilers, where steam is condensed back into water after going through the turbines and pumped back into the boiler, so it is feasible to treat the water to make sure it contains no impurities. This cannot be done in locomotives: where water is only used once, a great deal is consumed, and since these impurities remain in the water and cannot pass into the steam, they will accumulate in the boiler and must be removed somehow. Especially with 'hard' water, some of these impurities will stick to the metal surfaces inside the boiler and prevent heat passing to the water, and the metal can then overheat. Beyond a certain temperature, all metals will weaken and this is why boilers can explode. So it is important to prevent 'scale' forming inside a boiler, as well as removing 'sludge'.

Water presents a further set of problems. It is well known that steel will rust slowly if left in contact with water (even water vapour in the atmosphere); this 'corrosion' slowly eats it away. But there is another kind of corrosion: 'electrolytic'. Whenever two different metals are immersed in water which is at all acidic — (and in some places all tapwater is naturally acidic) — they form what is in fact an electric battery, a small voltage will be generated and one of the two metals will be slowly eaten away. The rate at which this happens depends on which two metals are concerned, and also on the strength of the acid. Copper and zinc, and lead and zinc, have a relatively high potential electric difference (and are used to make batteries). Steel and copper have a much smaller electric potential, but it exists all the same, and the most common form of electrolytic corrosion in the traditional British-type locomotive boiler, with a copper firebox and steel tubes and shell, is for small pits to be eaten into the tubes. These form around microscopic impurities in the metal, but can and do result in perforation and are the main reason why tubes need relatively frequent renewal.

Chemical treatment of the feedwater, which can also reduce the formation of hard scale adhering to metal surfaces, can reduce or stop the acidity of the feedwater, and so reduce corrosion of this kind.

However, all feedwater in practice contains some dissolved solids which will accumulate in the boiler, whether or not they form hard scale, and the chemicals added to treat the water also add to the total amount of dissolved solids. Water can only hold so much solid matter in solution; after a while the rest is 'precipitated' as sludge if not as hard scale, and if allowed to accumulate even sludge will cause overheating and damage. So it must be removed, either by 'washing out' the boiler or by 'blowing down' under pressure, using a special blow-down valve on the foundation ring, the lowest part of the boiler. Blowing down must be done as a rule several times a day, lowering the water level in the gauge glass 'half a glass' or 'quarter of a glass' as a rule. To avoid causing damage by sudden local cooling, 'washing out' is either done when the boiler has cooled naturally, which means the locomotive is out of service for a couple of days, or (to speed things up) using an ample supply of hot water. The intervals between washouts depends on local circumstances, and can vary from every three or four days to once a month or so, depending on the composition of the feedwater. The chemicals used in water treatment must also be balanced to suit the water supply, and in hard water districts it is often advantageous to have a water treatment plant to treat the water before it is used. Specialist advice is needed.

Coal quality can also have effects on the boiler. Apart from the obvious ones of blocked tubes or burnt tube-ends, some coals (and oils) can have high proportions of some impurities, particularly sulphur, which can cause problems of honeycomb pitting or excessive corrosion and erosion, if chemical composition is wrong.

Details of design are important to get right. Remember the first version of the Comet jet airliner, which had windows with square corners — very nice to look out of! But an airliner body is a pressure vessel, like a locomotive boiler, and

Tube 7" to 10" internal diameter
Length 3'0" to 4'6"
Material:- Rolled ⅛"- ¼" M.S
Plate with welded seam

Sets screws for adjusting immersion of tube feeder in tender

2 ⅝"dia holes drilled diametrically opposite at 4" to 8"distances apart.
Holes to be tapped and fitted with plugs.
The required set of holes to be left opened for the dispensing of treatment

Disc welded in end

Plug hole for flushing through feeder

FIXED TYPE

ADJUSTABLE TYPE

Above:
Sketch showing types of briquette tube feeders for one method of applying water treatment chemicals.

Right:
Some problems likely to occur with poorly designed boilers with too short girder bars and barrels with lap joints or single strap butt joints.

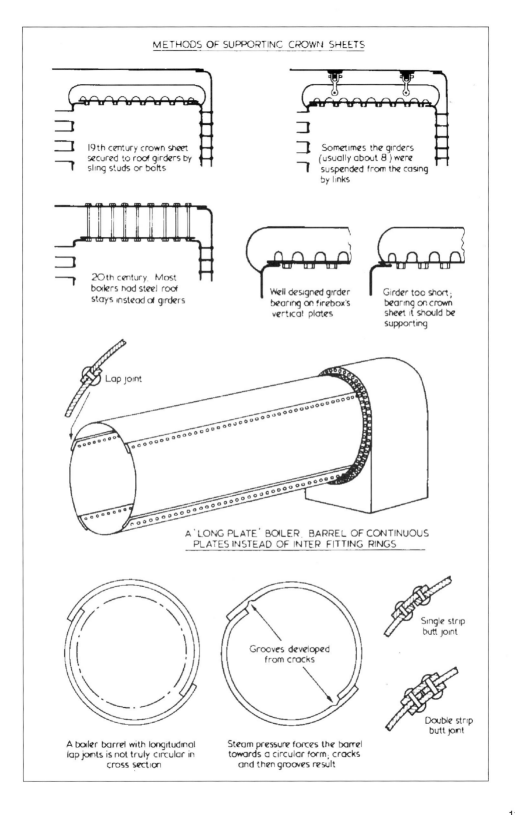

METHODS OF SUPPORTING CROWN SHEETS

19th century crown sheet secured to roof girders by sling studs or bolts

Sometimes the girders (usually about 8) were suspended from the casing by links

20th century. Most boilers had steel roof stays instead of girders

Well designed girder bearing on firebox's vertical plates

Girder too short; bearing on crown sheet it should be supporting

Lap joint

A 'LONG PLATE' BOILER. BARREL OF CONTINUOUS PLATES INSTEAD OF INTER FITTING RINGS

Grooves developed from cracks

Single strip butt joint

Double strip butt joint

A boiler barrel with longitudinal lap joints is not truly circular in cross section

Steam pressure forces the barrel towards a circular form; cracks and then grooves result subject to the same sorts of stresses and strains which can lead to metal fatigue and failure. The designers of the Comet had overlooked the concentration of stresses around square window corners, and many people lost their lives as a result. Experience taught some hard lessons about steam boilers in the 19th century: one of them, for example, was the mistake of joining two metal plates together in the obvious way, by laying one above the other and joining them with a line of rivets. As pressure built up, the two plates would tend to pull apart: this produced a stress at the riveted joint tending to pull the two plates into line with each other, and therefore tending to bend the metal at the seam weakened by the rivet holes. Metal fatigue resulted, all too often followed by a devastating explosion. (See diagrams pages 11 and 46.)

The problem was solved by keeping the two plates in line with each other, and joining them with an external metal strip riveted to each plate. This replacement of a 'lap joint' by a 'butt joint' prevented the bending strain which caused the problem. Modern practice often uses welding instead of rivetting, but dissimilar metals cannot be welded and so rivets are still used.

In conclusion is perhaps the most important point of all. It has already been pointed out that the usual cause of boiler explosions is overheating and therefore weakening of part of the boiler. The part most exposed to this risk is the top of the firebox, or 'crownsheet'. It is kept at a safe working temperature only by being covered with water. If the water level falls too low and uncovers the crownsheet a very dangerous situation immediately arises. It is therefore important that the crew always know what the water level is. Originally, boilers were fitted with 'try-cocks' at different levels, to test whether steam or water came out when they were opened. Unfortunately, hot boiler water instantly flashes into steam on reaching the atmosphere, so it looks the same: it just *sounds* different to steam coming out of a trycock. The difference is not easy to detect for many people, so as a precaution in dealing with a matter of life and death, trycocks are not beyond criticism (although some railways used them to the end of steam). Water gauges, where the actual water level is visible through glass, are much better: but they can also give false information unless the passages leading to them are kept clear of scale and blockage. Two or three times a day, therefore, it is vital to clear these passageways, one at a time, by using the cocks provided to blow steam through them.

These points all need to be remembered by locomotive users. There is one more thing, which should give some comfort. The law requires every boiler to be insured, and inspected annually by a qualified inspector. At intervals he will require a Hydraulic Test, in which the boiler is completely filled with water and then pumped up to a pressure 50% above its normal working limit or 25% above plus 10lb/sq in. This should be a maximum, particularly for a rivetted boiler, and do not be brow beaten by an inspector who wants a higher pressure; it only places unnecessary strain on seams, etc. Any leaks are then visible, and if anything breaks it will not result in an explosion. A hydraulic test is a very satisfactory safety measure as it will show faults without taking the pressure above that of normal working as excess pressure only strains everything unnecessarily.

2   **Boiler Mishaps**

When water is heated it expands and when it boils and becomes steam it occupies 1,728 times the volume, so that unless it can escape, as in a kettle, a pressure is created. When the early engineers tried to harness this phenomenon to power machinery they did not have reliable materials with which to make boilers, nor did they understand what was happening to the plates of the boiler under pressure, so that many true explosions took place, where the boiler literally tore assunder.

Although it is known that several of the early boilers exploded, the first recorded locomotive boiler explosion occurred in 1828 on the Stockton & Darlington Railway, and only four months later the boiler of the famous *Locomotion No 1* exploded at Aycliffe Lane, now Heighington station. These early boilers were mostly constructed by blacksmiths who had little experience or knowledge of exactly what was involved in constructing a vessel to contain steam under pressure and the effects

this repeated stress was having on plates. By the end of the 19th century a lot had been learnt but, more importantly, regulations had tightened up on the construction and operation of boilers, with steel of reasonably reliable quality becoming available so that design and construction was adequate for the work they were required to do. But maintenance was still somewhat lacking, as those instances will show.

At the turn of this century there was a partial firebox collapse on an engine which we know today as a Class J15, which showed how the power of steam escaping through a firebox produced a Catherine wheel effect. In 1935 on the Paris Lyon Midi Railway in France a real classic of this nature took place, due entirely to a boiler running short of water over a summit, and there were two cases of boilers actually exploding due to incorrect fitting and assembly of safety valves without proper checks of their functioning being made.

The boiler of a Great Eastern Railway Class Y14

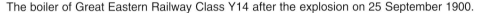

The boiler of Great Eastern Railway Class Y14 after the explosion on 25 September 1900.

(LNER 'J15') on 25 September 1900 at Westerfield, Suffolk, rocketed over a level crossing, rebounded off the track and landed on the platform some 40 yards ahead of the engine. The entire left side of the firebox had blown off the stays; there had been problems with bulging and instead of restaying with larger-size stays, the plates had just been forced back with a heavy hammer, and the stays (which were hollow) re-expanded and caulked, giving very little hold.

A Lancashire & Yorkshire 0-8-0 losing its boiler six months later near Knottingley was a similar case to the GER 'Y14', but with the additional feature of poor design including stays of an alloy of Hoy's invention.

It was on 21 April 1909 that the boiler of Rhymney Railway No 97, which was an eight-month-old boiler, exploded and was hurled about 45 yards. The Ramsbottom Safety Valves had been removed to remake the joint and in reassembling them the fitter had put all the

Two views of the aftermath of the Buxton boiler explosion, 11 November 1921. *IAL*

Detailed views of the Buxton boiler explosion. Top to bottom: The top of the firebox backplate; the firebox wrapper plate; the firebox crown and girder bars. *HM Railway Inspectorate*

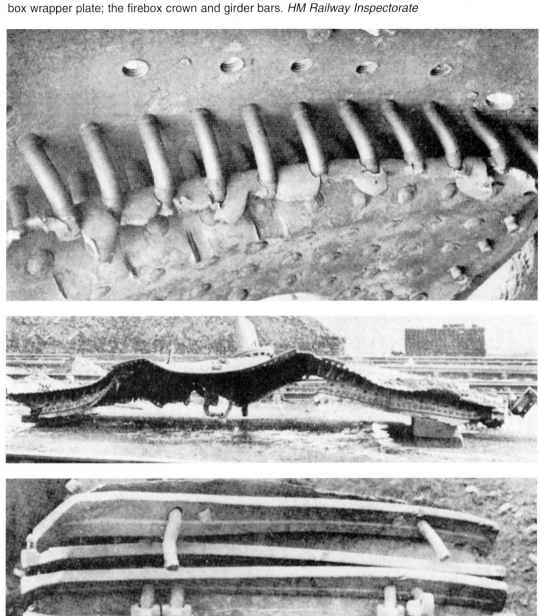

washers on the top of the lever and effectively screwed the valves down solid.

The driver who had taken charge of the engine was apprehensive that the pressure gauge was standing at 200lb/sq in — it should have blown off at 160lb/sq in — but the foreman, without checking, sent the engine to take up its working. After going a mile the injectors refused to work, so the driver returned the engine to depot, where the gauge glass burst and the catastrophe took place before the fire could be dropped.

The final example of this type was at Buxton on 11 November 1921, when the boiler of London & North Western Railway four-cylinder compound 0-8-0 No 134 exploded. To overcome the post war backlog of locomotive repairs, engines were sent to a number of firms and this one had gone to a firm in Glasgow, who had returned it only in July 1921. It had run only 2,600 miles, but there had been several reports that the pressure gauge was defective, whereupon it had been changed, but as there was no shut-off valve for the gauge, this could only be done when the engine was out of steam. The fact that there was nothing wrong with the gauge would not show and LNWR sheds did not have master gauges or means of connecting them — usually to gauge glass drains — to compare readings.

As can be seen from the picture, this boiler literally tore asunder in a true explosion. The cause, again, was solid safety valves, but in this case it was a cold morning and the valves were made of gunmetal on a gunmetal seat, which expands twice as much as cast iron, of which the body of the valve was made. The wings of the valves had also been machined much too tight in the body. A boiler of the same type was tested hydraulically and only started to give way at 600lb/sq in, so it must be assumed that the explosion occurred at somewhere around this pressure.

The importance of care in doing any work on safety valves or any pressure-sensitive item cannot be over emphasised, but, above all, when any work is done on safety valves their proper operation should always be checked afterwards. Moreover, no supervisor, however hard pressed, should ever accept any story relating to the pressure safety of a boiler without making a check for himself; these cases would not have happened if there had been proper supervision.

Everyone who has worked with steam knows that there is a great reserve of pressure in a boiler even after the fire has gone out. This is not only because of the volume of steam, but also because as the pressure reduces some of the remaining water boils off into steam — a fireless boiler is charged with water as well as steam. Whilst at atmospheric pressure water boils at 100°C, at 200lb/sq in it boils at nearly 200°C. As the pressure reduces more steam is created, so

The boiler of PLM No 141C623 lying about 512ft from the chassis.

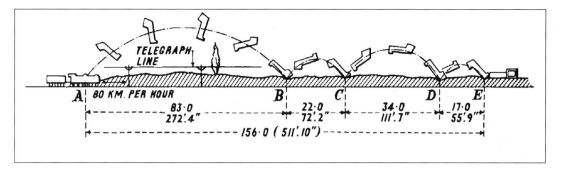

Above
Trajectory and minimum rotation of boiler blown from PLM No 141C623.

Below:
Fortunately the catastrophic boiler failures of the Victorian era are now rare but this example is included as a salutary reminder of what can go wrong if design and construction is not right. *LPC*

that there is a tremendous reserve of energy in a boiler from the water boiling off to form more steam, albeit at a lower pressure.

Although fortunately there have been no more major explosions like these examples in this country, there have been other spectacular ones in America and elsewhere. One of the most remarkable examples occurred on 2 August 1935, when the firebox crown on PLM 2-8-2 No 141C623 split down the centre, the boiler cart wheeling 512 feet across the fields, having cleared the telephone wires. Amazingly the chassis did not derail, but of course brake pipes were broken and the 609-ton train came to rest just over a quarter of a mile down the gradient. The crew were killed, so quite why they allowed the boiler to go short of water, plugs to drop, and continue over the summit exacerbating the condition, is a mystery, but from reconstruction of the evidence they must have had the crown-plate uncovered for 10 or 11 minutes. It is interesting to note that the firebox was made of steel and although some of the welds had been bent down, not one actually failed.

With the design and construction of boilers becoming generally sound, the failures that have taken place over the last 100 years can all be said to have been largely due to poor operation or bad maintenance, sometimes, as at Gettysburg recently, a combination of them both. Most present-day explosions have been of the firebox crown, or side plates, pulling over stays, the escape of steam through the stay holes usually

Above:
No 2557's copper firebox right hand side as bulged by the explosion at Bevois Park. The steam escaped through 52 stay holes when the plate was pulled off the stays: had the plate split the boiler would certainly have been destroyed. Note the foundation ring at the base of the firebox. *BR*

Left:
A view into the firebox, lying on its side, showing the bulged right hand plates. *BR*

being sufficient to release pressure before the plates completely failed.

During the war USA 2-8-0 Austerities were loaned to the railways before going to Europe. These engines have one Klinger reflex water gauge and three test cocks on the driver's side. These are excellent gauges and are to be commended. On the American Austerities these gauges were connected to the boiler by screw-down valves, the top valve being located on the top of the firebox and connected to the gauge by a copper pipe, with a wheel operating the valve through a universally jointed rod about 2½ft long. These valves only needed one complete turn from open to shut, but if not fully open could lead to false readings in the gauge glass; the long rod was not conducive to

Above:
The outer wrapper of the firebox showing the outward bulge after the stays parted. *BR*

Left:
The fire box outer casing after removal of the inner copper firebox, showing the corroded right hand stays which initiated the boiler explosion. *BR*

easy operation and could become very stiff in the bearing. Three of these engines suffered collapsed crown sheets whilst working in this country; in two cases the top valve was not fully open, one requiring two hands to turn it. The third case was a mystery as both enginemen were killed and no errors could be found.

The purpose of this booklet is to try to show some of the problems which can occur with boilers and how they should be rectified. These examples illustrate the consequences that can occur when maintenance or operation is not what it should be. Finally, I am illustrating a case of bad maintenance and inspection that was far short of what it should have been.

In 1949 the firebox of ex-London, Brighton & South Coast Railway Class E4 0-6-2T No 2557 burst inwards at Bevois Park Sidings, Southampton. A total of 137 of the 207 copper stays of the right-hand side of the firebox had broken, so that the copper side plate of the firebox bulged and forced it over the heads of 52 other stays which allowed the steam and water to escape with explosive force. The enginemen were blown out of the cab and severely scalded, but recovered, and the engine remained on the track with its boiler.

The stays were so badly corroded that in some only about one sixth of the original cross-section was left. It was thought that a group of about 15 parted first, throwing additional strain on their neighbours and a cascade failure took place.

The engine had been working at Horsham until about three weeks beforehand, where the water was very corrosive to copper. It was six years and 90,000 miles since the engine had had a general repair, but the boiler had been looked at by a Boiler Inspector only a month previously and he had declared the boiler fit for a further six months service. From what he must have seen, and knowing the effects of Horsham water on copper plates and stays, his decision was extraordinary.

Most of these examples are taken from the late C. H. Hewison's *Locomotive Boiler Explosions* (1983), a book which should be on the shelves at every locomotive depot and should be read by those responsible for boiler maintenance as well as footplate crews. C. H. Hewison was a Doncaster trained loco man, then became a Shed Master before going to HMRI as one of its inspectors.

3   Locomotive Boilers: Some General Points

In recalling practices from the heyday of British Railways steam, reference has been made to two books, and other documents: E. A. Phillipson — *Steam Locomotive Design Data and Formula* (1936) and E. C. Poultney — *Steam Locomotion* (1951), together with *Instructions for testing Examination and repair* as revised by CME Doncaster, June 1949, and MP 11, BR 87264, also HS(G)29 as well as some relevant Proceedings of Institution of Locomotive Engineers.

Even after nationalisation the old Regional practices of the London & North Eastern, London Midland & Scottish, Great Western and Southern Railways continued at the main works until virtually the end of steam and the sheds continued much in the same way for the engines with which they were familiar. There can be arguments today as to whether one method or another was right, but British locomotive boilers were extremely well constructed and maintained, which is why they have survived for so long.

For anyone completely unaware of what to do, D. W. Harvey's *Steam Locomotive Restoration and Preservation* makes very useful reading, and, if you can find a copy — and there are quite a few about — the instructions relative to boilers issued by BR LMR CM&EE Dept, Derby, revised as recently as 1959 has many details.

BR and its main constituents had their own standards and specifications for boiler construction and materials. There was BS931 produced in 1951, somewhat late in the day, for locomotive-type multitubular boilers of riveted construction, now out of print. BS2790 for shell boilers, which specifically states it is not for loco type boilers or riveted construction, is nevertheless used as a guide along with BS5500 by some insurers when considering design approval.

The laws applying to railway locomotive boilers have always been somewhat sparse: most boilers come under the Factory Acts, which do not apply to railways other than their workshop premises, but Her Majesty's Railway Inspectorate (HMRI, now part of the Health & Safety Executive), who controls the activities of most railways, require that all boilers are properly examined and maintained, and that they have proper insurance. The all embracing Health & Safety at Work Act, 1974, imposes many liabilities and responsibilities on any employer or operator of virtually anything, and clauses of it relating to plant apply to boilers, and can be certain to catch anyone who does not operate and maintain a boiler properly.

The Pressure Vessels & Transportable Gas Containers Regulations, 1989 No 2169 is important. These are being revised in 1999, but there is no change of significance to the chapters relating to steam boilers. Section 4(2) states that pressure systems shall be properly designed and properly constructed from suitable material so as to prevent danger. Section 5(5) states that the pressure system shall be provided with such protective devices as may be necessary for preventing danger, ie boilers must have adequate safety valves to prevent excess pressure building up. Although these regulations refer to 'mobile systems', this term does not include locomotives, to which the regulations do apply.

Section 5: Suppliers and manufacturers, also anyone modifying or repairing any boiler, shall provide written information concerning design, construction, examination, operation and maintenance as may reasonably be required for these regulations to be complied with. These people shall ensure that the following information is indelibly marked on the boiler, or on a plate attached to it: manufacturer's name, date of manufacture, the standard to which the boiler was built, maximum design pressure of the vessel and the design temperature. However, as 'standards' for loco type boilers are difficult to establish, this item may be difficult to comply with.

Section 8: The user shall not operate the system unless he has a written scheme for the periodic examination by a competent person of the pressure vessel, its protective devices, and any parts of the associated pipework which may give rise to danger. A competent person is one who has knowledge of the pressure system, normally the boiler inspector. This written scheme will specify the nature and frequency of examination, and will specify any special measures necessary to prepare the pressure system for safe examination, other than those that would be reasonable to expect the user to take.

Section 9: Covers the preparation and submission of reports by inspectors, including specification of repairs (if any) required to be done.

The Health & Safety Booklet *Locomotive Boilers* HS(G) 29 under revision in 1999 is itself a revision of one in which the Association of Independant Railways and the Association of Railway Preservation Societies were involved in preparation several years ago. Its purpose is to provide guidance on the practical applications of regulations made under the Health & Safety at Work Act of 1974. It amplifies some matters in this booklet, and should be essential reading in conjunction with it.

HS(G) 29 gives emphasis on the importance of examination, testing, repair and maintenance of boilers being carried out to an adequate standard, which requires the choice of suitable persons both to carry out these functions as well as supervise them, including the keeping of records

The boiler for the replica LNWR 'Bloomer' is of a size comparable to an London, Midland & Scottish Railway '4F'. Designed to BS2790:1969 it was welded by the Babcock organisation, who are welding pressure vessels all the time. The throatplate and doorplate, with their ogee bends were a problem successfully overcome by Roger Pridham. *Birmingham Railway Museum Trust/Alan Wood*

of days in steam, examinations, repairs and maintenance, including washing out. These repair records should include all details of materials used, their origin and specification, as well as details of contractors and personnel, including qualification certificates of all welders. For this purpose Responsible Person(s) should be properly appointed within each organisation, who should not only have knowledge of locomotive boilers, but also authority regarding their use; he must if necessary prohibit the use, even raising of steam, in any boiler if there is any doubt as to its safety.

The importance of the competent person — boiler inspector — having full experience of loco type boilers is very much stressed, and it emphasises that the choice of insurance company may be dictated by the organisation's experience with locomotive-type boilers — not only their examination, but also their repair. It is also important to be sure as to whether the contract with the insurance company is purely for inspection for insurance purposes or for inspection for the carrying out of necessary repairs.

Reading the railway press and journals of some organisations, I do question the economics of spending vast sums — six figures in some cases — on patching up these old boilers. The materials of these boilers

The completed boiler and firebox shell stands in the welding shop at Babcock, welder George Gray giving an indication of the size of the unit. *Alan Wood*

are practically all far beyond the age of anything that would have been in normal commercial service. Boiler maintenance and renewal is probably the most expensive single item of expenditure on a locomotive, yet boilers are treated with less care and concern by most people, probably because they are the least understood. How often have people told me that they only occasionally use an engine. When they say that between duties it just stands in the shed, full of water, I am afraid I am very critical of them.

Boilers do not like being warmed up and cooled down, far better if they are warmed up, kept as warm as possible and used every day, only being cooled gently for wash out, then warmed again and used. The main line companies at some of their larger more modern depots, put in hot water washing out plants, where the hot water and remaining steam was blown back into settling and holding tanks. The actual washing out was done with very hot water and clean hot water used for refilling, so that a locomotive only

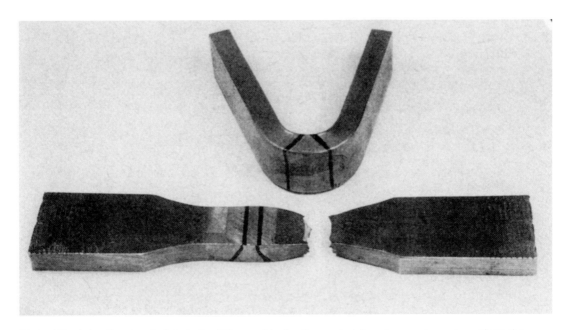

To test the integrity of materials in the 'Bloomer' boiler the material and procedures as well as the competance of the welders, test pieces were prepared. As can be seen the material failed before the welds. *Babcock Construction*

had to be out of service for three or four hours and saved all the stress and strains of cooling down and heating up.

The latest technology in Switzerland is to keep the boiler hot with electric immersion heaters aided by extra heavy insulation and lagging. I know this may not appeal to the enthusiast, who loves to see different big engines on each train, but do they pay the bills when the boiler plates have become too thin from corrosion and have cracked and have to be replaced? The chassis and mechanical parts can be painted and oiled and greased; the outside of a boiler, tubes and some internals, can be painted — when new and each time the lagging is renewed, wire brushing and two coats of aluminium paint are strongly recommended — but this treatment has only limited life. The best way to treat a boiler not being used again for some time is to blow it down hot, after pressure has virtually gone, remove all plugs and mud doors so that air can circulate, and keep it in a warm dry place like the National Railway Museum or a desert. If left outside rain will get in under the lagging and will create bad corrosive conditions. The presence of

coal dust or wet ash in contact with metal produces corrosion very quickly.

The smaller locomotives — particularly the narrow gauge — are getting new boilers, usually mostly welded. *Tornado's* new boiler is estimated to cost £250,000 sums of half that are being spent in patching up some of the old boilers, with no guarantee as to how long it will be before further large sums have to be spent. Once the principles of modern design are established, the details for different boilers to fit various classes will not require too much work, but co-operation is essential.

A steam locomotive boiler, consisting as it does of a rectangular firebox rigidly attached at its bottom and back to the rest of the boiler, is an inherently very unsatisfactory pressure vessel. All of its flat surfaces have got to be supported in one way or another to stop them trying to become spherical, which is the natural shape for any pressure vessel as a balloon illustrates. The cylindrical surfaces are in plain tension, but all the flat ones are trying to bend, as well as being in tension. The firebox, whether of copper or steel, is subject to the intense heat of the fire

Sectional view of a saturated boiler

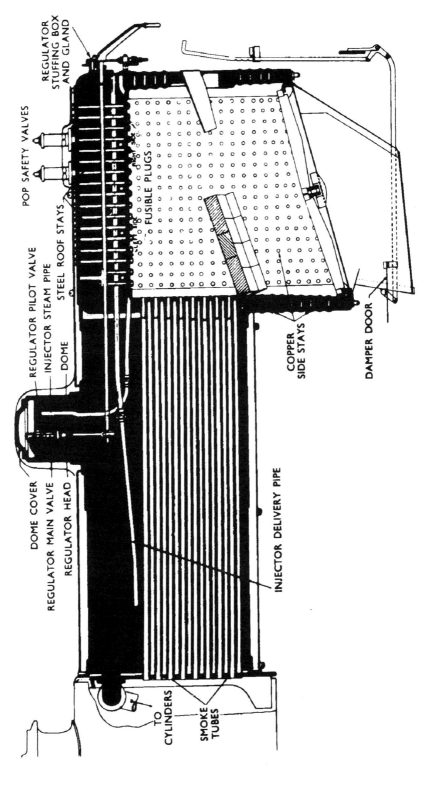

REGULATOR STUFFING BOX AND GLAND

POP SAFETY VALVES

REGULATOR PILOT VALVE

INJECTOR STEAM PIPE

STEEL ROOF STAYS

DOME

DOME COVER

REGULATOR MAIN VALVE

REGULATOR HEAD

FUSIBLE PLUGS

COPPER SIDE STAYS

DAMPER DOOR

INJECTOR DELIVERY PIPE

TO CYLINDERS

SMOKE TUBES

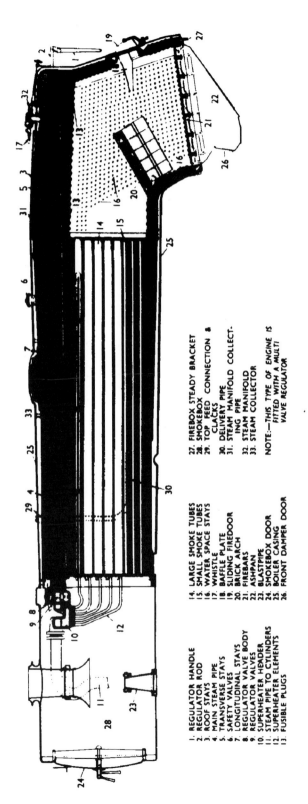

1. REGULATOR HANDLE
2. REGULATOR ROD
3. ROOF STAYS
4. MAIN STEAM PIPE
5. TRANSVERSE STAYS
6. SAFETY VALVES
7. LONGITUDINAL STAYS
8. REGULATOR VALVE BODY
9. REGULATOR VALVES
10. SUPERHEATER HEADER
11. STEAM PIPE TO CYLINDERS
12. SUPERHEATER ELEMENTS
13. FUSIBLE PLUGS

14. LARGE SMOKE TUBES
15. SMALL SMOKE TUBES
16. WATER SPACE STAYS
17. WHISTLE
18. BAFFLE PLATE
19. SLIDING FIREDOOR
20. BRICK ARCH
21. FIREBARS
22. ASHPAN
23. BLASTPIPE
24. SMOKEBOX DOOR
25. BOILER CASING
26. FRONT DAMPER DOOR

27. FIREBOX STEADY BRACKET
28. SMOKEBOX
29. TOP FEED CONNECTION & CLACKS
30. DELIVERY PIPE
31. STEAM MANIFOLD COLLECT-ING PIPE
32. STEAM MANIFOLD
33. STEAM COLLECTOR

NOTE:—THIS TYPE OF ENGINE IS FITTED WITH A MULTI VALVE REGULATOR

Sectional view of a superheated boiler

when working hard, and therefore expands and contracts more than the boiler itself, so that the plates suffer heavy stresses, and the supporting stays at the top front have to flex considerably. Various means are adopted to give these stays some flexibility, but the plates are still fully constrained at the firehole. Also the boiler is wracked and shaken about as it is rigidly held at the smokebox and restrained by the very solid clips at the firebox. The chassis is far from rigid and any twists in the track will be passed to the boiler, all adding to the many stresses and strains to which it is subject by its own operations. These wrackings and shakings can be far worse if the track standards are poor; bad track not only damages springs and mechanical details but boilers as well.

Operators can do much to minimise some of these stresses by the way the firedoor is opened and by careful use of the blower when there is little fire but the boiler is hot. It is very important to warm up a cold boiler as slowly and gently as possible. Wherever possible it is best to put a fire in the day before the engine is going to be used which will slowly warm the boiler throughout. It is raising the temperature from cold — which may be only 10°, or even less in winter — to boiling, 100° (and double this at full pressure), right throughout which can cause the most stress and strains. If the firebox has a sloping grate, make sure that there is some fire right down the front to warm the bottom section of the firebox. It also helps not to clean out the fire completely at the end of the day; closing the dampers, filling the boiler with water and putting a lid on the chimney will help to keep the boiler warm. Even with small boilers there are often enough glowing embers in the morning to start a fresh fire.

Unless there are facilities to wash out a boiler with hot water, it is most important that cold water is not applied to hot plates. If cooling down must be speeded the best method to cool a boiler down is to feed cold water slowly through an injector into the hot water, if possible using one of the special cooling down valves which control the flow of water into the boiler. The feed is connected to an injector overflow pipe and a special plug put into one of the backhead plugholes with a hose to a suitable drain. The rate of flow should start very low, depending on the size of boiler, but about five gallons a minute for the first two hours, 12 gallons a minute for the second two hours and 25 gallons a minute for the final two hours is a guide. Even if the special valves are not available, it is not difficult to attach a hose to an injector overflow, and make a plug and length of hose to drain the water away. It is important, particularly to start with, that the flow of cold water in is kept very low.

Of course it goes without saying that the water supplies should be tested, and in all probability treated. If the water is at all hard and is not treated, hard deposits will be made on the heating surfaces, which can cause tubes and plates to overheat and will have to be removed as far as possible at washout. Railways in moorland areas generally have soft water, but this is often acidic, and whilst it does not leave hard deposits can be very corrosive. In both cases the chemical treatment will produce soft products which it is essential to get rid of by blowing down. It is important that a programme and regime is laid down for this, including where it is to be done.

It is very important if water treatment is used, that the process is closely and regularly monitored by someone who has good experience of what he/she is doing. It is probably better to blow down and wash out regularly, particularly where a locomotive is using varying waters (eg on main line runs) but is going cold anyway. Having said this, where locomotives are in daily use, chemical treatment is important, and therefore staff must be trained to monitor the water composition and check on blowing down, etc. A 'dirty boiler', or one with excessive amounts of suspended solids from treatment can be liable to prime, that is carry water over into the cylinders. This can wash away lubricating films and can considerably impair operations, apart from the danger of breaking cylinder covers, pistons, etc.

Power stations have special facilities for continually analysing the boiler water and varying treatment accordingly. Supplies can vary, particularly after heavy rain, so that regular testing of the water is very desirable.

4   Locomotive Boiler Construction

Traditionally British loco boilers were of riveted construction with copper fireboxes. There is a British Standard Specification for these, BS931 of 1951, which is no longer available, although BR and its main constituents had their own standards and materials specifications. It is anticipated that any new boilers will be largely welded, to the original general design; BS2790, for shell boilers of welded construction, can be used as a guide, although it is stated that it is not suitable for locomotive boilers.

The simplest boiler gives saturated steam and has a 'round top' firebox. The 'round top' refers to the outer firebox: the inner firebox still has a flat, and very slightly curved, top. There are many of these on both the standard and narrow gauge; the ubiquitous 'Austerity' ('J94') 0-6-0s, Brighton 'Terriers' as well as 0-6-0 tender engines are examples. The GW, in particular, favoured the Belpaire type of boiler, with the outside virtually following the shape of the straight-topped firebox inside.

The steam in the boiler is only at the temperature of the water, and although its temperature does rise as the pressure increases, once it leaves the boiler and starts to do work it starts to revert to water and cease to perform any useful function. To make the steam perform like a gas, it is superheated, and to do this it is passed through superheater elements, which are situated in large flue tubes through the boiler barrel. Superheated steam can expand and do more work in the cylinders, and so the engine can work at a short cut off, saving a very considerable amount of fuel on any but the very shortest of runs, although there are additional costs with the superheating equipment.

Modern main line locomotives may have round-top or Belpaire fireboxes, and they may have narrow fireboxes to fit between the frames, or wide fireboxes, which are somewhat shallow, and extend over the frames. Wide fireboxes are only possible where the driving wheels are relatively small — Class 9F 2-10-0s — or there is a small carrying wheel at the rear — Pacifics, 'V2s', Atlantics etc.

The Belpaire firebox is supposed to give better steaming because it is wider at the water surface, and allows a greater steam space at the hottest part of the boiler. Since the inner and outer plates at the top of the Belpaire firebox have the same contour, the stays can be more direct and square to the plates and also of the same length. The construction is altogether more flexible and leads to fewer problems with roof stay breakage. It is more expensive to make, although where bulk manufacture is concerned this disparity is less.

The parallel boiler barrel was the traditional form, but most larger modern boilers are of conical or taper form so as to give greater steam space at the hottest part nearest the firebox and to reduce the variation in water level over the firebox crown on gradients. Once again it is slightly more expensive to construct; apart from the difficulties of rolling a cone, if it joins to a parallel ring, the end has got to be rolled parallel to make a joint. The taper boiler does save weight at the front of the engine. The old Festiniog Fairlie double-ended boilers were peculiar in this respect in that although they appeared to taper in elevation, they were parallel in plan, the top being cylindrical but inclined, and there being a triangular flat area on the sides.

Traditionally, British locomotive fireboxes have been copper. It is heavier and more expensive, but does conduct heat better and does not wear or corrode so rapidly as steel. Copper and steel fireboxes were of riveted construction but modern practice has been to weld steel fireboxes; though welding has been used on copper, particularly to allow the building up and replacement of worn areas, the process is much simpler for a steel firebox, which is now becoming more common.

Most modern larger boilers include a combustion chamber. This increases the firebox heating surface, which is the most important heating area, improves combustion, and reduces the temperature and thus the burning of the tube ends, although with the tubeplate being set forward into the barrel the tubes are less accessible for attention.

A few engines, Bulleid Pacifics being noteworthy examples, are fitted with Thermic Syphons. These give greater heating surface in the fire, and additional support to the brick arch in a wide firebox, as well as helping to circulate water from the bottom front of the firebox to the crown, which gives useful additional flow of water over the crown even if the water level is low.

Staying

With all the flat surfaces of the locomotive-type boiler, there has got to be more than adequate support to the flat surfaces, as the strength of the plate is only sufficient to support itself for a relatively small area. This strengthening can take different forms, but is known as staying.

The sides of the firebox can be stayed inner to outer directly. The fireboxes are solidly locked together at the bottom by the foundation ring, and at the back by the firehole ring. Copper expands more than steel, but the inner firebox is subject to the heat of the fire, and whether made of copper or steel expands upwards and forwards. The stays therefore have to flex, and to withstand this they must be made of appropriate material, with the screw thread a close fit in the plate. The central portion of the stays must be turned down to the root diameter of the thread, and this also reduces the tendency for scale to adhere and makes it easier for it to be removed at washing out; also, very importantly, turning down the central part of the stay to a smooth finish removes any tendency for cracks to start at the thread root.

Stays can be of copper, steel or Monel — a nickel/copper/manganese alloy — but in all cases tensile strength plus ductility is important. They are normally screwed 11 or 12tpi and it is essential that not only are the threads a good fit, but they must be the same form so as to be watertight. To best achieve this, copper stays are normally riveted over, but steel stays are only caulked outside (hence the necessity of a properly fitting thread) and on the inside are nutted, with thin nuts. These nuts are sacrificial, and when they burn away can be replaced. The stay must not protrude through the nut, and the nut must be made with a countersink inside so that the outer edge of the nut is in contact with the plate.

Stays may have a hole — ⅛in or slightly larger - through or partly through. This is to provide a tell-tale sign if the stay breaks. The solid end (if provided) should be outside so that steam and water does not escape into the lagging; the objection is that the inside holes can become blocked by burnt ash, etc. But they are considered to be an aid, as if there is any doubt a drill will soon clear any blockage, and if the stay is broken, steam or water will show in the firebox.

This should not be confused with the practice of providing a fairly large hole in the end of the stay, into which, after the stay has been screwed in, a drift could be hammered to expand the end of the stay to make it steamtight.

Roof Stays

Some of the older small boilers may still have girder or roof bars to support the crown of the inner firebox. These are obviously only suitable for round-topped fireboxes where the wrapper is cylindrical and therefore not needing support. These girders have ends machined to fit onto the front and back of the firebox, between they will sit well clear of the firebox crown to allow water to circulate; it is essential that these spaces are kept clear and this is one of the weaknesses of the system. The girder bar may have lugs at each stay point or loose distance pieces may be used, but the firebox is secured to the bar with long set screws. The advantage is that all can be assembled before the firebox is put into the boiler, but if the set screws or loose distance pieces allow the stays to become loose, replacement is very difficult — we had to do it on the Festiniog on one of the Fairlies. It is not unknown on older boilers to have a mix of girder bars and direct staying. This can induce a permanent set in the firebox crown since the girder bars allow the

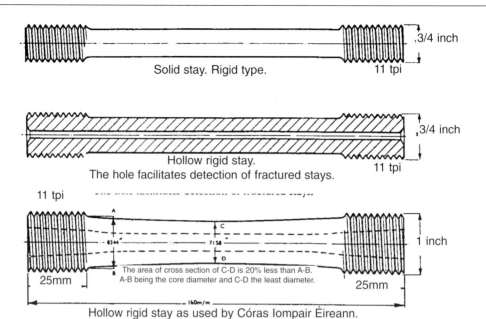

Solid stay. Rigid type.

,3/4 inch

11 tpi

Hollow rigid stay.
The hole facilitates detection of fractured stays.

,3/4 inch

11 tpi

11 tpi

1 inch

25mm

25mm

The area of cross section of C-D is 20% less than A-B.
A-B being the core diameter and C-D the least diameter.

160m/m

Hollow rigid stay as used by Córas Iompair Éireann.

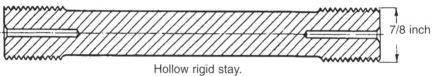

7/8 inch

Hollow rigid stay.
This type has the greater strength of the solid stay combined with the flexibility of the hollow stay.

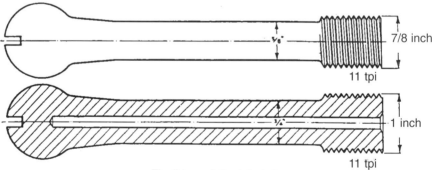

7/8 inch

11 tpi

1 inch

11 tpi

Flexible or Articulated stay.
These may be either solid or partly hollow. The threaded end is fitted in the usual way. The other end forms part of a ball and socket joint.
Note the difference in dimensions as between solid and hollow stays.

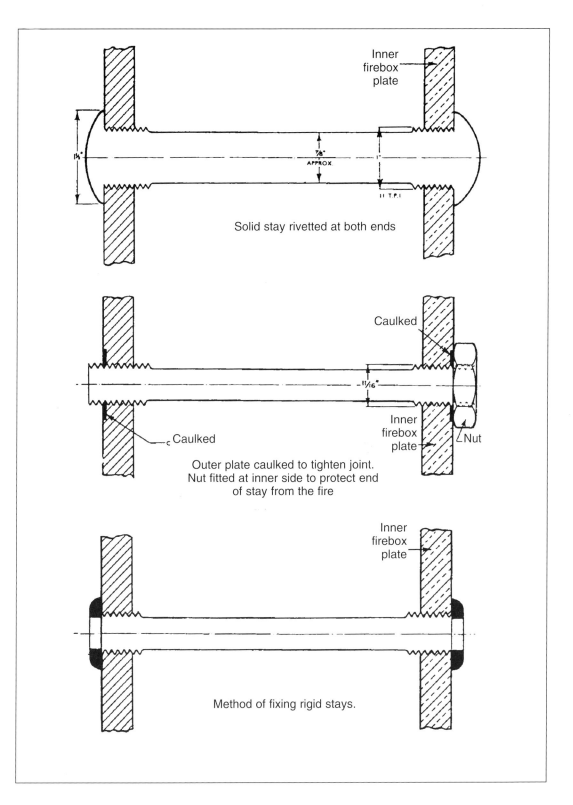

Inner
firebox
plate

$1\frac{1}{4}$"

$\frac{7}{8}$"
APPROX.

1"

11 T.P.I

Solid stay rivetted at both ends

Caulked

$1\frac{1}{16}$"

Inner
firebox
plate

Nut

Caulked

Outer plate caulked to tighten joint.
Nut fitted at inner side to protect end
of stay from the fire

Inner
firebox
plate

Method of fixing rigid stays.

firebox to expand upwards (can be ⅛in) whereas the directly stayed area will be held, making the crown appear to be bulging in the area of the direct staying.

The modern Belpaire boiler can be simply stayed with long stays from firebox to wrapper. They are usually nutted on the inside, but some may be riveted over, depending on practice. The outside can be nutted or riveted.

With the round-top firebox, staying can be direct, in which case the firebox crown is usually slightly curved so that the stays can be radial to the crown but not at too acute an angle through the wrapper. They are usually nutted inside the firebox but the outside can only be riveted. To give more flexibility at the front, where the stays may get into compression in some circumstances, there can be 'T' slings hanging from an angle riveted to the wrapper. A stay passes through each arm of the 'T' and is nutted and pinned, for security. The bottom end has a long square which, when the firebox is put in, will protrude through the stay holes, the square enabling the stay to be screwed in tight, and then nutted. Sometimes these stays have an enlargement on the water side with a cone face to screw up tight to the plate and some engines have this method for all crown stays. I will only comment that I have never found boilers to be precision made, and particularly after years in service, I wonder how such stays are made and fitted so as to give reasonably uniform support to the firebox crown.

With steel fireboxes, and sometimes with copper, flexible stays are used. These still require the stay to flex at the firebox end, but as they are ball ended — and with a certain amount of freedom — will not be put into compression, and the ball end can swivel in all directions. The socket for the ball end can be screwed into the wrapper or welded and have a steamtight cap.

Longitudinal and Palm Stays

Some boilers have stays running above the firebox and tubes from front to back. These are usually screwed and nutted at the back end, and nutted both sides at the smokebox tubeplate. Palm stays go from the firebox tubeplate below the tubes and are made of a forged bar. Machined at the end with a threaded portion, a

copper stay is screwed in from the firebox side into the palm stay, then riveted over in the firebox. The other end of the palm stay is forged larger to rivet to the barrel.

There are many ways by which the large flat surfaces of the front tubeplate and the backhead of modern boilers are given additional support; angles being riveted on and then long stays taken to another bracket riveted to the barrel are common.

Transverse Stays

Belpaire outer fireboxes, particularly, with their flat sides above the inner firebox, have to be supported between the firebox stays and top radius. This is done by stays going across from side to side above the inner firebox. They are usually screwed and nutted.

Foundation Rings

British practice is to forge these, others use cast steel. Some reduce the water space above the foundation ring, in which case care must be taken that sludge does not accumulate at the bottom. Foundation rings should be double riveted at the corners where leakage is most likely to occur.

Firehole Ring

This is another sensitive area fixing the inner and outer fireboxes together. The forged or cast ring is simple, but is too rigid for larger boilers, where the plates of the inner and outer fireboxes are flanged so that they can be riveted together with corner welds inside and out.

Welded Fireboxes

With the development of welding techniques, the practice became increasingly used, particularly in America and Europe, for steel firebox repairs, then for complete fireboxes, and now the all-welded boiler. In this country Bulleid pioneered the practice with his Pacifics, which have all welded fireboxes and the wrapper is welded to the throatplate.

In all cases a similar basic shape has been used, except that instead of flanged and riveted overlaps the plates are similarly flanged and formed, but butt-welded together.

Today there is increasing difficulty in getting plates flanged and formed to the old shapes. Not only have the flanging blocks and presses gone, but so have the people with the necessary skills. Some smaller fireboxes are being constructed with one sheet for sides and crown with the same radius for the corners, and then the tube plate and doorplate welded inside this, with corner welds inside and out.

Alternatively, it is not difficult to flange corners in sections and then weld these sections together, as was done by Schweizerische Lokomotiv- and Maschinenfabrik (SLM) for the boilers for the new rack tanks built for various mountain railways in Switzerland and Austria.

Staying can be as described earlier, or stays can be of a suitable bar welded in. It is best if the hole for the stays is counterbored to half depth and then fully welded. Flexible stays are usually necessary for the front rows of larger boilers.

With steel fireboxes it is usual to seal weld tubes at the firebox end — see below. Copper welding — this is mainly used for repairs to firebox plates — see maintenance.

Tubes

Brass and copper tubes were used extensively in the past, but they are only very occasionally used today. They are expensive, but they do offer resistance to pitting and corrosion from the

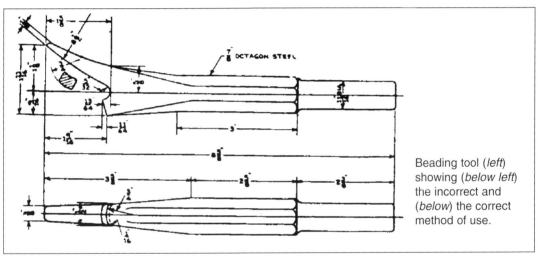

Beading tool (*left*) showing (*below left*) the incorrect and (*below*) the correct method of use.

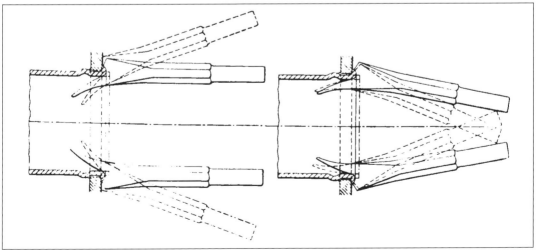

Above:
An early example of a welded firebox design seen here on a Southern Railway 'Merchant Navy' boiler. Note that whilst the firebox is welded the barrel is of traditional rivetted construction.

Right:
New rack locomotive boilers showing flanging produced in sections and then welded together. *SLM*

Below:
All welded boilers awaiting completion of the fireboxes. *SLM*

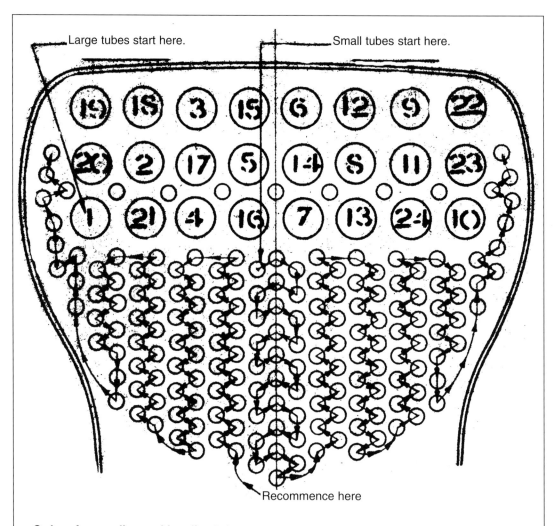

Order of expanding and beading tubes.
The large tubes are to be expanded first, starting at No 1 and working in numerical order as shown, then beaded in the same order and finally tightened up with the expander. The small tubes are to be done in a similar manner, following the order shown by the arrows in the diagram. The small tube placed among the large ones to be done last.

Above:
The order for expanding and beading tubes as specified by Doncaster Works.

Above right:
Diagram of tubes expanding and ferruling as specified by Doncaster Works.

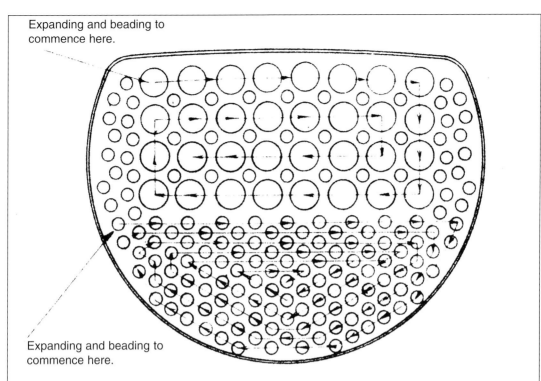

Expanding and beading to commence here.

Expanding and beading to commence here.

Order of expanding and ferruling tubes.
The large tubes are to be expanded first, starting at the top and working round in the order shown by the arrows, then beaded in the same order and tightened up with the expander. The small tubes are then expanded similarly as shown by the arrows and afterwards ferruled in the same order. The small tubes placed among the large ones to be done last.

S

chemical characteristics of certain feed waters. Iron tubes have also been used. Copper and brass tubes give the problem of electrolytic action accelerating local corrosion of the steel plates, but also, when they get thin, they can collapse or fail completely, whereas steel tubes normally develop leaks giving warning of impending failure.

It is normal to expand tubes into the firebox tubeplate, whether the firebox is of steel or copper, by means of roller expanders. These expanders should have five rollers at least; some expanders only have three rollers, and these are apt to simply distort the tube, as it will tend to straighten out again between the more widely-spaced rollers, and therefore fail to seat properly in the tubeplate. It is an advantage if

the expander is of slightly larger diameter on the inside, or waterside, of the tubeplate, although this is not universal. Once expanded sufficiently to stop any leaks, the tube is beaded over using a special beading tool, bringing the tube end into contact with the tubeplate as close and smooth as possible, to avoid the end of the tube being burnt away. With steel fireboxes, the tube should then be lightly seal welded on the outside of the beading; this should be done with the boiler full of water, and from bottom to top each side. The reason for this additional procedure with a steel firebox is that since copper expands with heat more than steel does, a copper firebox will tend to grip the tube more tightly as the boiler heats up, which is why tubes tend to leak in a steel firebox if not seal-welded.

Superheater Flues

These are almost always of steel, although copper was not unknown. It is usual for the firebox end to be swaged down for about a foot, the smokebox end being slightly enlarged, to facilitate insertion and, particularly, removal, when encrusted with scale, etc.

Fixing at the firebox end can be by screwing in with a fine thread — 10-12tpi — or they can be grooved and expanded. In both cases they should also be beaded, and in steel fireboxes seal-welded as for small tubes.

In no cases should any tube be other than seal-welded as removal will be extremely difficult and stresses will be set up in the tube bridges which will lead to tubeplate fractures as well as making it difficult to clean up the hole properly for the new tubes to be fitted. At the smokebox end all tubes should only be expanded. It is important to expand tubes in a regular order. With a simple saturated boiler, start at the top left-hand corner and work round the outside going round until you reach the centre, to ensure you do not miss any, mark them as they are done. For a superheated boiler do likewise for the flues, then the main nest of small tubes, finishing up with the small tubes amongst and beside the flues. See diagrams.

FITTINGS WITH A SAFETY CONNOTATION

Safety Valves

Older locomotives are usually fitted with Ramsbottom Safety Valves. The disadvantage of them is that they progressively open and close, and will very often 'dribble' until the pressure is well below normal. The spring between the two valves is set slightly off centre so that one valve opens first. The tail of the lever enables the valves to be 'tweaked' to stop dribbling by means of a gentle tap, but if it is the front valve that is dribbling it will need to be a very small tap upwards.

For overhaul, all that is needed is a grinding in of the valve, and at the first steam test adjust the setting of the valves to blow off at the correct pressure by means of the nut and lock nut on the top.

Comparison of a 3in Ross valve with two 3in Ramsbottom valves of approximately the same discharge capacity.

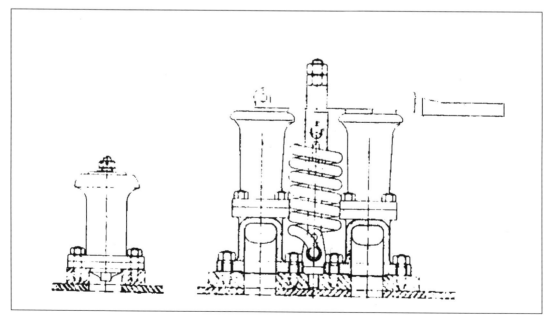

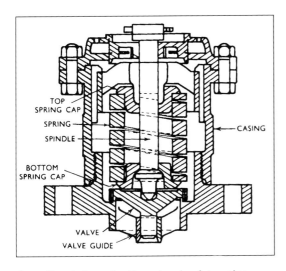

A sectional view of a Ross 'pop' safety valve.

Labels in diagram:
TOP SPRING CAP
SPRING
SPINDLE
BOTTOM SPRING CAP
CASING
VALVE
VALVE GUIDE

Small narrow gauge locomotives may have one, occasionally two, spring-loaded safety valves. These need similar maintenance to the Ramsbottom type.

Today the Ross 'pop' valve is more or less universal, many of the older locomotives having been modified for its use. A Ross valve occupies much less space, and is much lighter, than a Ramsbottom valve. Any safety valve must be mounted direct on the boiler with no intervening valve or pipework. Due to the importance of maintaining correct proportions and clearances, it is important that maintenance of the Ross valves is carried out only by people with the proper skill and experience. In old railway days this was a main works job, sheds were not allowed to touch them other than exchange old for new on the boiler.

Fusible plugs

It is a British requirement that at least one fusible plug be fitted in the crown of every firebox. Fusible plugs are similar to washout plugs, but with a large hole bored through, which is filled with lead. The hole should have recesses bored in it to give a better key for the lead — 99.97% pure — and it must be clean and well tinned before filling. There are also proprietary fusible plugs in which a ball or pellet is, in effect, soldered into the body, but these are only rarely found in locomotives, mostly on industrials.

Fusible plugs should be removed at annual inspections and closely examined. Any scale or ash should be removed, and if there is any doubt about the core, the plug should be replaced. Plugs should also be examined at washout as far as possible. They should be renewed completely at any major boiler overhaul as brass tends to crystallise with heating and age. Proprietary plugs may be screwed in on a parallel or taper thread, so when replacing them make sure that the correct type and fit is obtained. The main lines each had their own standards, some taper, some parallel, and of differing tpi. The British Railway's Standard adopted the London, Midland & Scottish and Great Western Railways parallel plugs with 8tpi, these were increasingly being fitted to other engines as fireboxes needed replacement or plug holes to be altered. It is most important that the correct type of plug is used for the hole. Make sure that the plug is not screwing in against something; on smaller boilers longitudinal stays can sometimes be over the plug hole and the plug can screw in against the stay.

With most types of plug as the threads get worn the hole is tapped out a size larger and then the appropriate size larger plug must be fitted. Maximum sizes were laid down, whereupon the hole was permanently plugged and a new hole drilled between neighbouring stays; this was a main works task and they had standard positions according to size of locomotive and number of plugs. Derby's 1959 instructions give the following:-

(i) where one fusible plug was originally fitted at the centre of the crown plate:

The new position must be as near the centre as adjacent stays will permit and equidistant from four adjacent stays.

(ii) Where two fusible plugs were originally fitted at diagonal corners of the crown plate:

If only one plug has to be repositioned it must be

Above:
A fusible plug showing the softer plug centre.
National Railway Museum

Right:
Diagramatic drawings of fusible plugs.

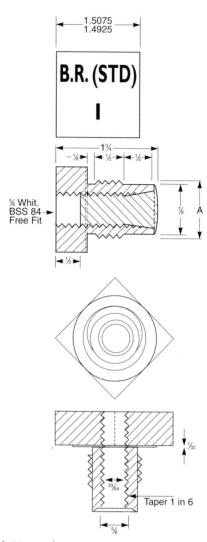

Not to scale

Item No	Nominal Size	Dimension A	
		Limits	
		High	Low
1/SL/SW/88	1⅛	11270	11250
2/SL/SW/88	1³⁄₁₆	11895	11875
3/SL/SW/88	1¼	12520	12500
4/SL/SW/88	1⁵⁄₁₆	13145	13125

as near the original position as the adjacent stays will permit and equidistant from four adjacent stays.

If both plugs require repositioning they must be inserted on the opposite diagonal and equidistant from four adjacent stays.

(iii) In both cases of curved crown plates where two plugs are fitted on the longitudinal line:

The new positions must remain on the centre line but moved forward or backward, the mini-mum distance adjacent stays will permit, and be equidistant from four adjacent stays.

There is controversy as to the need for fusible plugs; when an engine is working and a fusible plug goes, the loco crew may not be aware of it, and there have been many cases where the fire-box crown has overheated to such an extent that it has forced itself over the crown stays, the resultant escape of water and steam ejecting the fire, bursting through the ashpan in the process, as at Gettysburg in 1995 and several other cases.

No 46224 *Princess Alexandra*, for the second time in its life, had a bad blow in the firebox coming south in 1948 at Carstairs, which a foreman and two fitters from the shed could not locate, as with a hot fire they did not see the steam. A few miles further on at Lamington, the firebox crown pulled off 24 stay heads. Another incident caused by the use of LMS coupled water gauge cocks.

Pressure Gauge

Every boiler must be fitted with a pressure gauge which must be checked for accuracy every year against a master gauge. It should be connected to the boiler through a length of pipe, usually ⅜in copper, with a shut-off valve where steam is taken from the boiler. It should be situated where it can be seen conveniently by the fireman, and is visible by the driver. The blowing-off pressure should be indicated on the dial by a red line.

Water Gauges

Every boiler must have two means of determining the boiler water level, preferably both of these will be some form of transparent type of gauge, but a set of three test cocks is an acceptable alternative to the second gauge.

The simple glass tube between two fittings has been in use for very many years, but with the modern boiler, where the front of both wrapper and firebox is made as high as possible, the gauge glass can, in fact, give misleading information. Design data says that when the water level shows at the bottom of the gauge glass, the crown sheet of the firebox is well and completely covered when the locomotive is descending the most severe gradient it can encounter in service and/or is standing on a curve having maximum super elevation. In fact, many modern large locomotives have fireboxes where the front fusible plug is 10 feet from the gauge glass, and with the water just showing in the bottom of the glass the plug is only covered by one inch of water. Going up a 1 in 100 gradient the front plug will have no cover, and loco men must be trained that on a steep gradient a good level of water — ½ to ¾ glass — must be maintained to ensure adequate coverage of water of all of the crown of the firebox. After passing over a summit, particularly if a down grade follows, the water goes to the front of the boiler, and the crown can become uncovered (see the photo of what happened to PLM No 141C623 in 1935).

Gauge glasses must be fitted with a protector, the glass of which should be of a thick safety pattern. The back is a spring loaded 'door' which automatically closes when the protector is put in place. A practice to be highly commended is the painting of these back plates with alternate diagonal black and white stripes. These appear to reverse behind the water, so that anyone looking at the gauge is in no doubt as to whether the glass is full or empty. There have been many mistakes, including some nasty firebox explosions, due to footplate staff mistaking an empty glass for a full one; it had been London & North Eastern Railway practice for every backplate to have these markings, and it is significant that on the LNER and subsequently BR, no ex-LNER locomotive was involved in any serious boiler explosion reported to Her Majesty's Railway Inspectorate.

The top and bottom fittings should be fitted with balls which are supposed to shut off the steam and water if a glass breaks. They rarely do, but I recall one incident when they did: there was a bang and then silence and it took some seconds for it to be realised what had happened.

LMS engines were fitted with shut-off cocks which were at 45° when open (or shut) with one handle on the upper cock, which was connected to the lower cock by a link and arm. The advantage was that if a glass broke, the long handle could more easily be pulled down and both cocks shut off in one go. The disadvantage was that the portways could not be tested separately when the engine was in steam, which was the cause of more than one firebox collapse — as recounted under fusible plugs.

MP 11 states that on boilers with a working pressure of over 200lb per square inch, gauge glasses should be renewed at washout every three to five weeks on Western Region engines; for boilers at lower working pressure this renewal should be at seven to nine weeks. Depending on usage, these old practices are a useful guideline.

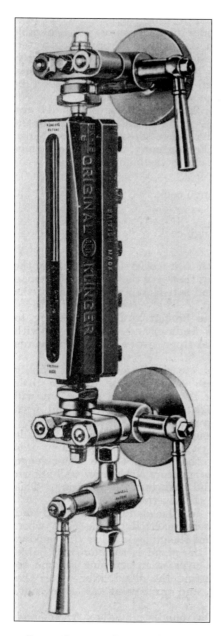

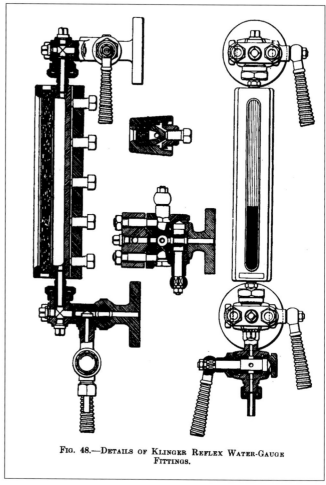

FIG. 48.—DETAILS OF KLINGER REFLEX WATER-GAUGE
FITTINGS.

Left:
Klinger reflex water gauge.

Above:
Details of Klinger reflex water gauge.

Every three to five weeks the passageways through the cocks should be checked by passing a rod no more than ⅟₁₆in in diameter, or similarly 'across the corners' if square, through all passageways with the cocks open. With coupled cocks do this simultaneously through top and bottom cocks to ensure synchronisation. If not, the connecting link or handles must be adjusted. Klinger Reflex prismatic types are used on some engines, particularly on the smaller gauges where the driver is in close proximity to the water gauge. These gauges give very clear indication of the water level. They should be checked in steam, if not done so by footplate crews and if the joints are blowing the joints should be renewed. If the glass is pitted on the joint face it should be renewed; take care not to scratch the gauge glass.

In the days of BR the repairs allowed to be done at sheds was limited, though practices for this varied considerably from region to region, much after the practice of the old companies. If any serious defects developed, these were a main works task, and the engine was duly sent either for a special or casual repair, or, depending upon its mileage and general condition, for a heavier repair.

Circumstances today are different, the independent railways are fairly self contained, but many locomotives are independently owned. This is a situation which needs careful managerial supervision to ensure that work done on these independent locomotives is up to the standard required by the railway and, for the boiler, its inspection regime; often the engine can have different insurers and inspectors from that of the railway; operating and hire agreements must cover this precisely or there is risk of conflict and arguments arising.

New boilers

If being constructed entirely from original drawings, 'grandmothers rights' will apply but regulations are changing and the extent to which this may exist must be verified. Nevertheless, any regulatory body will have to give very strong valid reasons for not accepting a design that has

been in use on many boilers for a fair length of time. Most new boilers of necessity have to be modified in some ways from the original, even if all drawings are available, and therefore come under the Transport & Works Act and the design will have to be approved by HMRI. The design and calculations (or at least details thereof) will be checked by the competent person and probably his head office. He will then need to know who is to construct the boiler, and close liaison needs to be established and maintained between constructor, inspectors and purchaser to ensure that everything is done to specification and satisfaction, with checks on sub assemblies, welders and welding, etc. Inspectors have to be paid for this service, but it is better to get a good job done well to everyone's satisfaction, than to have a poor one which is not right, and then causes no end of arguments as to whose responsibility it is to put it right, ending up by paying solicitors fees.

When completed there should be a hydraulic test and, if possible, a steam test. This is when the clock starts to tick for further examinations, and if the boiler is not being put into use fairly quickly it is as well to discuss matters with the inspector beforehand to find his requirements for static hydraulic and steam tests during and after construction and then to start the clock.

A new all welded boiler for a 15in gauge locomotive. The original boiler lasted less than 10 years due to inadequate wash out arrangements. A classic case of inspectors, and insurance companies, not properly approving designs. *Alan C. Butcher*

5   Boiler Examination and Repair

The boiler of a locomotive tends to be the least understood part and this is probably because it is something unique to the steam locomotive. A number of people think that if it has been examined by the insurance company inspector — the competent person — both cold, at a hydraulic test, and in steam, then they can just start steaming away, but this is only a start, particularly if the boiler is not new. You may not be wanting to run over Railtrack lines, but to satisfy the main line authorities boiler inspectors must demonstrate regular and frequent involvement with fire tube locomotive boilers, and other knowledge and skills in such work. In engaging insurers and their surveyors, it is important that you make similar checks, as inexperienced inspectors can lead you into some very expensive repairs; all part of the reason HRA wanted to produce this book.

It is important that you make regular examinations of your boilers and carry out repairs, just as much as you examine the mechanical parts and repair them. Do not rely on the annual inspection, it is important that you have a 'Responsible Person' to make inspections, to arrange for repairs and to check on what has been done. It may be that you do not have anyone who has much experience of boiler work, in which case it will be necessary to contract in someone for the purpose, but you should be in the lead in carrying out any day-to-day repairs and in deciding upon major work which may need to be done. Major work should be done in consultation with the competent person: tell him what and how you propose to do the work and get his approval. Work with him, not against him, but remain in the lead.

The major examinations by outside inspectors — competent persons — are only one part of the important checks that must be made on boilers to endeavour to minimise the risk from defects which have occurred. What may start as a minor fault, if not attended to, can soon turn into a major disaster. The people who are first in the line for this are the operators, ie engine crews, and their proper training in best operation of the boiler can do much to prolong the boiler's life, as well as keeping it safe. The experience of footplate staff in knowing their various engines can be a great help in that they are most likely to spot that something is not right. If they see something and are not sure about it, further advice and assistance should be obtained.

When preparing an engine and disposing of it after it has been at work, look for signs of leakage of water from seams, rivets and tubes, both in the firebox and smokebox as well as as far as can be seen outside. Even if the source of leakage cannot be seen, its existence will usually be obvious either from steam leaking through lagging joints, and/or water running down and dripping somewhere.

Tubes should also be checked to see that they are not blocked, or covered at the ends with a crust known as a bird's nest. These can be raked down and any blockages cleared and the tubes swept out.

When an engine is coming in for wash out it should be examined beforehand whilst in steam by the 'Responsible Person' or some other suitably qualified person nominated by him. He will be looking for much the same things as at daily inspections, but with a slightly more experienced and technical eye. He will have to decide if any repairs or attention are required. After washout and before plugs and mud doors are replaced, he must inspect the inside of the boiler as far as possible to ensure that the washing out has removed all scale, dirt and sludge, and also check the firebox crown and the water spaces at the base of the firebox. Visible stays should be checked for necking, corrosion, pitting and wastage. Broken stays may be indicated by bulging of firebox plates, and doubts should be confirmed by hammer testing, a broken stay giving a very dull and dead response to a hammer blow. Today there are very few people who are regularly hammer testing stays and are therefore really competent at distinguishing between sound and broken stays. Even the most skilled inspectors doing it regularly were not infallible.

In recent years some electronic testing methods have been developed and are proving a very useful tool, though expensive. With oil-filled probes and careful use, they can give reliable answers to the problem. One or two of the larger railways are acquiring the equipment and the skill to use it and it may well be worthwhile for other railways to hire the equipment — and operator — to get reliable answers much more quickly than with a hammer. Unduly wasted stay heads, rivet heads and stay nuts should also be noted and recorded for future examinations to pay particular attention to them. The general condition internally and externally should be monitored, so that any sudden change in condition will be seen and investigated further, with possible remedial action.

Every year — technically every 14 months — the boiler must be examined by the boiler inspector. For this all mudhole doors and washout plugs must be removed and the firebox and smokebox thoroughly cleaned internally, as well as all visible external parts. The inspector may call for other parts to be stripped out, eg the brick arch, either before or during the examination. If this examination is satisfactory, or when any necessary repairs have been carried out to the satisfaction of the inspector, he may call for a hydraulic test, but in any case he will want a steam test, and this should be done no more than eight weeks later.

The opportunity should be taken, even if the inspector does not examine them himself, to check all mudhole doors and washout plugs for wear, corrosion and accuracy of fit: both the door or plug, and the seat or the threads of the hole it fits in. Make certain that the mudhole door bolt is secure and the threads are not corroded or worn.

The major examination at seven years, or such longer time as may have been agreed with the inspector, normally requires the boiler to be removed from the frames, all lagging and fittings removed, and all tubes and flues taken out. This enables the exterior and interior to be fully examined, and this is where experience is important. At this time it is essential that all work is done to ensure that the boiler will work satisfactorily for the period to the next major examination; it is a waste of time and money just to carry out minimal repairs to keep the boiler going. One of the most important considerations is plate thickness, generally and locally. If there is wastage, the amount and extent needs to be checked — 80% of original thickness is the normally accepted minimum, 75% locally is acceptable, but needs close monitoring. The bottom of barrels usually waste due to not having been drained and dried out properly, as do the firebox wrapper, throat and backplates just above the foundation ring. With the constraint of the foundation ring, there is often grooving in this area, and whilst small areas of wastage can be built up with welding, it is usual to cut out a whole area, and weld and rivet in a new section of plate. It is important that the new plate is of similar composition to the old, and if curved, the fitting is particularly important. The sequence of the welding must also be carefully arranged so that any tendencies to pull out of fit are restrained.

Some of the larger boilers have their own idiosyncracies, and it is important that these are known and watched for. The LMS used 2% nickel steel for their bigger boilers, and the shoulders on the radius of the backhead are a problem on many older large boilers. Before any welding is done make absolutely certain of the material composition of the area concerned.

Copper fireboxes can be allowed to burn away to 50% of original thickness between stays, but this is a minimum, and at a major overhaul there must be sufficient material remaining so that the plate will not get down to this limit of thickness before the next major overhaul.

In days gone by the standard method of repair of thin areas was by means of patches, and I have even heard of impoverished railways patching patches, but this is essentially short termism in extremis. Today, with the advance of welding techniques it is possible to weld in new areas of copper or steel, but it is important that it is all designed extremely carefully, and the work done by properly certificated welders to ASME 1X or BS287-288 standard. If this care is not taken plates will distort and residual strains and stresses will be left in the area of repair, which may then show up later as fractures. Do not try to be too economical with the patch, it is better to make it just that little bit larger, than have to come back a few years later to do a bit more. Remember that welding is not a process of sticking the pieces of metal together, it consists of creating a local pool of molten metal and as that pool contracts it tries to draw in the local parent metal, which is why pieces of unre-strained metal curve up. In a rigid structure like a boiler this must be allowed for both in the design and execution.

Copper can be welded, and the process was developed by some of the old works, particular-ly during the war when copper was in short sup-ply. Today there are specialist firms who can do almost as much with copper as can be done with steel, but it is expensive, and for some jobs,

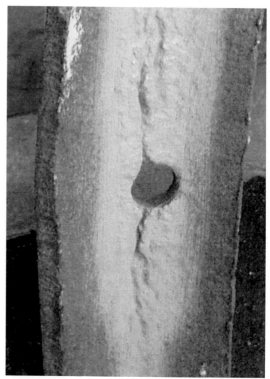

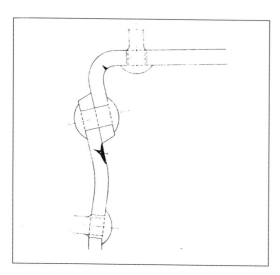

Above:
This diagram shows how the plates, where two are rivetted together, are trying to bend under pressure, so that fractures and grooving tend to develop after a time.

Above right and right:
Some examples of grooving wastage which are difficult, if not impossible to see without disman-tling the boiler; (top) Standard Class 4 backhead, (right) front tubeplate from GWR 'Dukedog'.

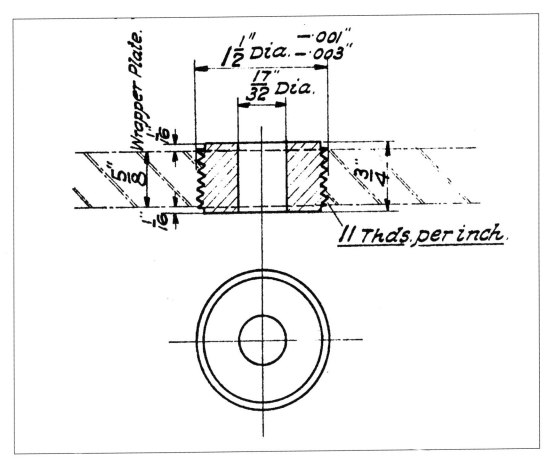

$1\frac{1}{2}''$ Dia. $\frac{-\cdot001''}{-\cdot003}$

$\frac{17}{32}''$ Dia.

Wrapper Plate.

$\frac{3}{16}''$

$\cdot010''$

$\frac{3}{16}''$

$\frac{1}{4}''$

11 Thds. per inch.

Standard stay bushes for steel wrapper plate.

requires the firebox to be positioned so that the work is down hand; much of it is done by actually creating a pool of molten copper, which will obviously not stay where wanted unless it is all suitably positioned. It is, however, very useful for building up worn flanges, and can be used for welding-in patches, avoiding the problems which do arise from double-thickness material when rivetted together.

When new stays are fitted, it is most important that the threads are a tight fit in those of the hole, and that the correct material is used. This will probably be specified on the original boiler drawings. As holes and threads get worn, stay sizes can be increased by tapping holes next larger size (an increment of $\frac{1}{16}$in is normal). If the

copper firebox is replaced, or partly replaced eg by new half sides, stays should be brought back to minimum size, and the hole on the steel should be bushed. Practices varied, some works allowed all stay holes to be bushed in side plates, others up to only 50%, although there were no restrictions to bushing holes in throat and back plates, except into or close to radii.

Body of oversize stays to be reduced to .01in less than core diameter of threads.

The normal maximum size of steel stays is $1\frac{3}{16}$in, but a limited number of $\frac{7}{8}$in stays were allowed in special cases.

Stay nuts should be $\frac{1}{2}$in thick and countersunk at 45° on faced side to depth of one thread. The projection of stay end will be not less than $\frac{1}{16}$in

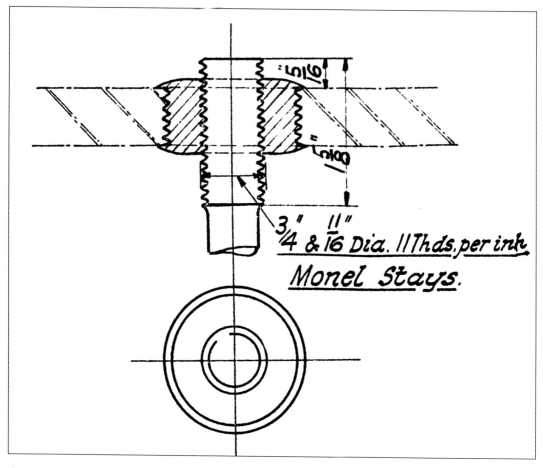

$\frac{3}{4}$" & $\frac{11}{16}$" Dia. 11 Thds. per inch

Monel Stays.

Standard stay bushes for monel steel stays.

or more than one thread. Nuts must be tightened up with a spanner not more than 6in long. When the stay end is worn it may be re-threaded ⅟₁₆in smaller and the appropriate nut fitted, but nothing smaller. If a steel stay cannot take a new nut it may be riveted, but these must be double-handed rivetted.

A split die should be used for cleaning dirty threads of direct stays.

Rivets will often have to be replaced due to wasted heads. The building up of rivet heads by welding is not advised. After the head has been cut off it may be possible to drive it out, but if the rivet had been well fitted it will have to be drilled out. New rivets must always be put in red hot;

they should be a tight fit in the hole and have to be knocked in tight, then held up whilst riveted up with a rivetting gun with an appropriate dolly. It is vital that this is all done quickly as the rivet will lose its heat to the mass of cold metal, but the whole process of rivetting, whether for boilers, structures or anything else is an old art which has to be maintained so long as there are boilers and structures requiring it.

Washout plug holes must be examined, and the threads cleaned and re-tapped, but care must be taken that this does not result in the plug going in too far, in which case the plug hole will have to be built up, re-drilled and re-tapped or just re-tapped a size larger. Make sure that

Diagram of a split die for cleaning direct stays.

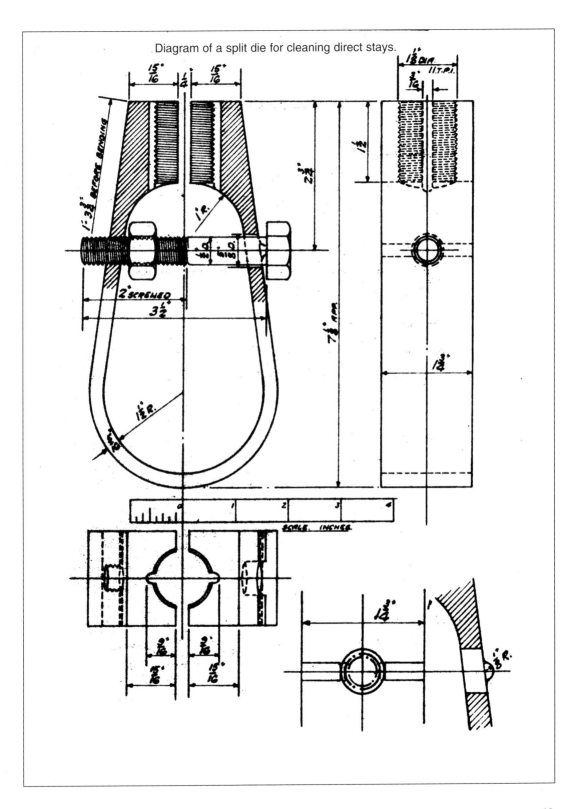

taps and plugs have the same taper and tpi as there are both 11 and 12tpi in use by different works.

Washout plugs should be cleaned and checked. They should be renewed at a general boiler overhaul, or after they have been heated for removal, as brass crystallises with age.

Mud door holes must be very carefully looked at to ensure that the edges of the plate are good and square, and that the jointing surface inside is flat. If not, building up must be done. The doors themselves must also be similarly examined to make sure that they are a good fit, there should be no more than ⅙in gap between the locating spigot of the door and the hole in the plate. Most doors are forged, but a few are made of plate, and these can distort and not fit flat on the boiler plate. The stems of mud doors also waste, and threads wear. These can be renewed, threaded into the door (usually 11tpi) and seal-welded or rivetted over on the underside. This is most important, as joint failures can ensue. It is important that the proper woven asbestos joints are used for this purpose, these are still obtain-

 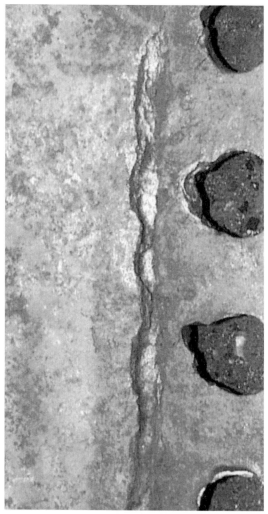

Examples of grooving wastage: (above left) Standard Class 4 backhead, (above right and right) South Eastern & Chatham Railway 'C' class outer firebox wrapper at foundation ring level.'.

able and are exempt from the chrysotile asbestos regulations at least until 2001 or until a suitable reliable alternative material is made available. Some people are reverting to the older method of jointing with lead, but do not forget that there are tight regulations on the use of this material particularly relating to its handling.

Whilst the boiler is stripped, opportunity must be taken to examine all the internal pipework:the main steam pipe and all the smaller pipes collecting and carrying steam for the various fittings, as well as those delivering water

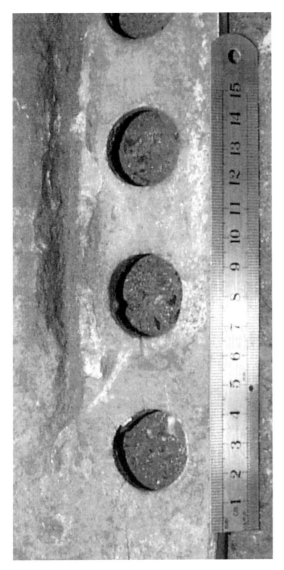

from the injectors. When the regulator is shut, for those engines with the regulator in the dome, the main steam pipe is subject to full boiler pressure externally. If it develops a leak, steam will continue to flow when the regulator is shut, and if the leak is of any magnitude this could lead to problems in controlling and stopping the engine. If, as is usually the case, the leak is at the bottom of the pipe, water will get into the steam when working, and add to the problems. It is better to take the pipe out, and thoroughly examine and test it whilst the opportunity arises, than let it go, necessitating stripping the dome and smokebox once again if it fails.

Whilst tubes can be re-ended and re-used, this is not recommended except in special circumstances. It is better to get a completely new set of tubes, but if there are some good ones they can be kept and re-used if patch replacement becomes necessary. Flues can be re-used if they have been carefully extracted and are still in good condition without pitting. Flues will have to have a new end welded on to replace that lost at both ends, where they have been expanded. This process is not recommended except where flues have only had very limited use and are in very good condition. Look out for internal pitting and corrosion, particularly if water has been used to clean them internally.

All fittings should be thoroughly checked and overhauled. This must include the careful examination of the body of fittings, which may well have suffered from wear and tear or even maltreatment. Spindles of valves will most likely be worn and probably bent, and require renewal. Once again it is far easier to do all this when the valve is off the engine on the bench, than to have to patch it up — or even take it off the locomotive — when problems arise later in service.

It is now 30 years since the demise of steam on BR, and far longer since steam was properly maintained rather than patched up to keep engines running during the transition to diesel. This is almost a working lifetime for most people, so that today there are few people around with good memories of the way repairs were done properly, and still less people who want to remember such things, and either work or help today. This makes it vital that we pick the brains of any who are willing to help, either who worked at sheds or who were involved in repairs at main works, and we must train younger people as much as we possibly can from these older people.

Some of the longer established railways have developed extensive workshop facilities, and are able to carry out considerable boiler repairs completely in house. The majority of boilers must go to one of the firms specialising in boiler work, or one of these railway workshops, or must bring in boiler specialists to do the work on site. Whatever way is chosen there is a considerable opportunity for problems to occur; the job specifications must be very clearly set out in agreement with the inspectors, and the inspection regime they will require must also be set out.

I am afraid that there are some firms in this business who think that they have more experience than they actually have, and there are far too many problems caused by firms doing the most outrageous things, and inspectors accepting it. The engine starts to be used, and leaks start to appear; how often do magazines contain accounts of boilers having to be stripped, sometimes not just once, because things have gone wrong? I am not going to say that engines never had to go back to works to have leaks put right, but it was rare on BR. Whilst everyone is arguing as to whose fault it all is, the engine that was wanted to earn money is sitting somewhere and solicitors probably have to be brought in to help, at more expense. Be very wary, modern high-tech welding etc can be very useful, but if wrongly applied by people who do not know locomotive-type boilers you may end up with worse problems than you started with.

I have already queried the wisdom of putting new wine into old bottles, or continually repairing old boilers, the plates of which are already fatigued and worn. This is particularly true if the boiler is on an engine which is intended to work hard and regularly, rather than a vintage machine only run for its historic connections — though some of these are being completely reboilered.

Whatever is done, it is most important that a rigid regime of inspection is instituted, both for the safety of operators and everyone else, but also to endeavour to prolong the life of the boil-er. A little care can save a costly repair and this applies to boilers even more than many other parts. If you do not have people with good experience of loco boilers in your organisation able to give continued supervision to the boilers, pay for someone from another railway to help and train your own people. This will be money well spent and as your own experience grows you will have to call on this help less and less.

The following set of illustrations were taken during the recent overhaul of *Flying Scotsman*. They show the sort of repairs which are becoming commonplace during major boiler overhauls.

1
A view of the copper backplate flange after removal of the seam rivets. Wastage and cracking of the plate is clearly shown.

2
Internal grooving on the inside of the backhead.

3
A close-up of the copper backplate showing how a number of rivet holes have split to the edge of the plate. A new flange piece will be welded to the original.

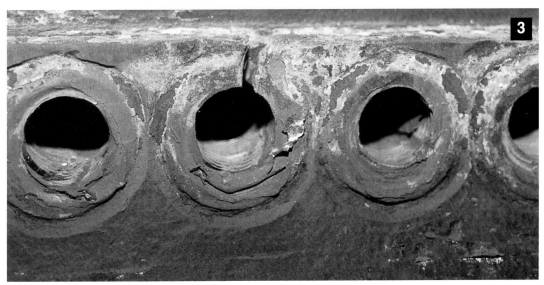

4
One of the two stiffening plates which are rivetted inside the boiler backhead. Note the grooving along the centre line to the plate fitted on the driver's side.

5
The grooving on the plate fitted on the fireman's side, the plate breaking in two when removed.

Index

The boiler and chassis of LMSR Pacific No 46229 *Duchess of Hamilton* under restoration at the NRM, York.

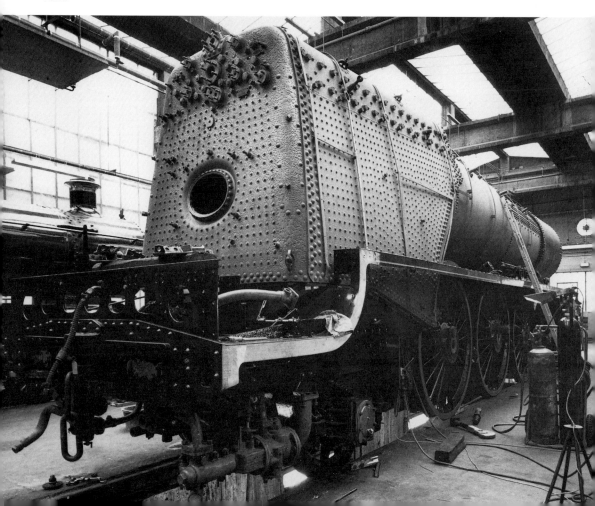